UNINTENDED CONSEQUENCES

E.C. HOPPIN

ISBN: 0615771637
ISBN-13: 978-0615771632

ACKNOWLEDGMENTS

This is a work of fiction and any similarities between the characters or events depicted in this novel and real life people or occurrences are coincidental.

I would like to thank Dr. Brett Bartlett for his assistance regarding forensic pathology and Dr. Ken Atchity and Beth Hauser for their editorial comments. I especially want to thank my wife, Barbara, for her patience and support during the writing of this book.

CHAPTER ONE

It was a typical St. Louis summer day, hot, humid, and the city smelled like yeast. The pungent smell from the brewery hung over the river city as though the Arch itself was spewing the contaminant into the atmosphere. Of course, Anheuser Busch kept St. Louis economically alive, so Carl shouldn't complain too much. Carl really liked St. Louis. Of course, he was born and raised here, so he didn't have a lot of other cities to compare it with. He did know one thing, though, and that was he would much rather be a cop in Missouri, the "Show-Me State," rather than in Illinois, the neighbor to the east which, particularly upstate, had the "I'll Show You" attitude.

Carl's temper was worse than usual because the piece-of-shit Crown Vic he checked out from the Missouri State Police motor pool stunk worse than the city and the air conditioner rattled and put out air no warmer than it was outside. At least the AC made the air inside the car move around a little.

Carl drove. He liked driving, and, fortunately, his partner Elwood Brannon, would much rather ride shotgun.

Carl and Elwood were as different as night and day. Nobody called Elwood by his real name. In fact, most of the people who knew him didn't even know his real name. He was "Mouse" to the rest of the world. One look at Mouse and you knew where he got the unflattering nickname. He was about 5'9" to Carl's 6'2", and Carl was jet black with a handsome face while Mouse was ashen, almost sickly looking, with thinning dull brown hair, a receding hairline, and a ferret-like face with the worst excuse for a mustache ever seen in the Western world.

But Mouse's looks were deceiving. He was a brown belt in martial arts and could easily flip a 220- pounder without even breathing hard. And he was smart, real smart.

The other notable fact that made Mouse a legend in the station house concerned his wife. Somehow he had snagged a knockout runway model with a body to die for, and she was absolutely devoted to Mouse. With her 5'11" frame, even without her ever present 3 inch heels, she towered over Mouse, but they didn't care. They had been married for 6 years, which Carl envied because he hadn't even made it to the altar yet.

There was nothing Carl Watson hated worse than being called out to investigate a DB—a dead body found at home. All he got from the dispatcher's fragmentary report was that a postman in rural St. Louis County noticed the mail piling up in the mailbox of some lady who had lived alone there for the past six or eight months. When the mailman went to knock on the door, the stench hit him like that time his old coon dog crawled under the house to die. After he upchucked in the neglected flower bed off to the side of the dilapidated porch, he called 911 and hung around for the cops to show up.

Carl got called because the DB was in an unincorporated area of the state in the jurisdiction of the Missouri State Police. As soon as he got out of the Vic, he knew the postman was right on. This was a DB, sure as God made little green apples.

The inside of the house was worn, but it was well kept, or at least it had been until the blood from the victim's head wound attracted enough vermin to keep an entomologist busy for a week. The question of the day was whether the lady fell and died of natural causes, or did some dude bash her brains in just for a few bucks?

As Carl waited for the Medical Examiner to arrive, he looked around. There was no evidence that the place had been ransacked. Everything was in its place, except for the upended chair underneath the bare light bulb on the ceiling of the small living room. Carl flipped on the light, but nothing happened. Then he noticed the empty sleeve of a 100 watt GE bulb next to the chair, and right beside that was a broken bulb which looked otherwise new. To Carl, who had been a cop for longer than he cared to remember, it looked all the world like an unfortunate accident, where the African American lady stood on the chair to replace the bulb, fell off, and hit her head on the edge of the oaken coffee table nearby. As Carl looked at the table, he could see old blood at the sharp corner of the table. He figured the ME would find some wood splinters in the gaping head wound. If so, that should make this an easy call.

"What do you think, Mouse?'

"What do you mean, what do I think? It's obvious what happened, Carl. We can wrap this one up by lunchtime. I may even have time to run home for a quickie."

"Don't go there, Mouse. It just reminds me how long it's been since I had a nooner. In fact, since I had sex at any hour."

Carl was bored, but he was also a really good cop. He loved his job,

2

even though it sometimes exasperated him.   Nevertheless, he was always thorough, so he began leafing through the lady's desk.

He found out her name, Missy McCain, and her age, 52.   There were lots of pictures in the living room, almost all of them photos of the same handsome man with the coloring of Starbuck's latte coffee, that sort of creamy black skin with nary a flaw.   Pictures of him as a youngster showed him in his football uniform or wearing his graduation gown.   In later pictures, Carl could see the man's life unfold—photographs of him wearing his Army dress uniform at a military celebration and in his combat gear surrounded by his buddies and even a few Arabs.   An array of trophies and memorabilia from growing up lined the wall, including an Easton metal baseball bat inscribed, "Little League Champions, American Division, 1984."   Carl hefted the bat and took a couple of practice swings.

"Probably the son, don't you think, Carl?"

"Yeah.   Obviously, the mom is real proud of the kid."   Carl would need to find out who he was so he could give the son the bad news.

In the second drawer on the left hand side of the small desk, Carl found a stack of spiral Mead notebooks, the kind that he used growing up in foster homes, and in a nearby closet he found another stack of notebooks going back years, each precisely numbered, one to fifteen.   Every page was covered, front and back, with the precise scrawl of someone used to preserving every scrap of paper, not to waste.

As Carl perused the early volumes, he noted the tentative handwriting of an unsure teenager, whereas later volumes bore the graceful, confident cursive of a writer who was much more self assured.   The words and the spindly, almost fearful, writing of the latest volume, however, gave Carl pause.   It was written as though the author had a premonition of an impending catastrophe.

Out of curiosity, Carl went to the first of the journal volumes.

Entry, September 8, 1970

I never thought I would be able to go to high school, but here I am.   The school isn't the greatest, with worn out buildings, even more worn out teachers, and kids from the Pruitt-Igoe projects, most of whom I know, since I grew up with them.   Mostly, though, I've tried to stay away from the kids at Pruitt because nothing good would ever come out of hanging around with them.
They look as defeated as the rest of the place.

I got really lucky.   My teacher is Miss Washington, a new teacher, so she isn't as beat down as the rest of them.   I think Miss Washington likes me

3

because she asked me stay after school. She told me that she thinks I have lots of potential, but I will need to work extra hard to try and get out of Pruitt-Igoe. That's why I started my journal. Miss Washington said a journal would help me learn to express myself better, and it would help me organize myself. We'll see.

Carl skipped ahead. Obviously Missy McCain had taken that advice 38 years earlier to heart, since she had years of her life religiously recorded in her journal.

Entry, September 30, 1971
    What did I do to them? Those boys kept bullying me, saying, "You think you're better than us. Bullshit. You're just another stupid nigger girl like all the rest, good for just one thing. And that stupid journal ain't going to mean shit when we got you down begging for more of us." I didn't beg for more. I begged them to leave me alone. I want to tell somebody what happened, maybe Miss Washington, but what can she do. She'll probably think I asked for it. That's what most of the girls do. They like the sex, but I'm not like most of the girls. Miss Washington can't help. I'll just have to deal with this myself.

Entry, June 28, 1972
    The noise in this place is driving me crazy. As soon as I started having cramps, I knew that I needed to go to the hospital. I wish someone could go with me, but I stopped going to school when my belly started getting bigger. I didn't want to disappoint Miss Washington, so I just stopped going. She came to see me at Pruitt-Igoe, but I told her that I couldn't go back to school when I looked like I did. The boys who raped me told me that if Miss Washington came around anymore, they were going to hurt her too, so I told her I didn't want to see her again.
    I never saw a doctor during my pregnancy, but I knew that the only place I could go when my baby came would be St. Louis City Hospital, because that's where all the poor people went.
    The baby ward is one big room with about 15 beds along each wall. There are no individual rooms, not even any curtains, so I can hear 30 girls crying and screaming, all of them swearing they are never going to have sex again. And then there's me, who didn't even have sex the first time. Just got

4

raped.

The nurses and doctors remind me of Carver High School teachers, all of them except Miss Washington. They are overworked, bored, and uninterested. They do what's necessary, but nothing else.

Entry, July 8, 1972

My cramps finally went away, but it still hurts where the Indian doctor cut my stomach to take my baby out. He said I couldn't have my baby the usual way, so he had to cut me.

I couldn't understand why the nurses brought me different babies. One was so sweet. All he did was suck and sleep. Another one they brought in never stopped crying. It seemed like they were so different. Why can't my baby act the same all the time?

Entry, July 15, 1972

The nurse finally explained to me that they had to cut me because I had more than one baby. That's why the babies act so differently, they were different. I don't know how I can take care of one baby all alone, let alone more than one.

My stomach feels better. I am going to sneak out with my sweetheart baby. Surely, the hospital will take care of the other.

Carl reflected on what Missy McCain had written thirty-six years earlier, primarily because he had often wondered what his own biologic mother must have felt when she left him behind. In the black community it was not unusual for there to be an absentee father, but the matriarchal culture usually dictated that the mother or grandmother looked after the children. Over the years, Carl had occasionally considered searching for his biologic mother, but he had never taken the time to follow through. Now, as he read her words, Carl could almost sense the heartbreak and fear which Missy must have felt when she made the decision to leave part of her family behind, knowing that to do so would perhaps improve the future for all of them. He wondered what circumstances prompted his own mother to make the same choices as Missy McCain.

CHAPTER TWO

Carl was convinced this was just an unfortunate accident, so he let the CSI guys go. They had lots of other crime scenes they could be working on—real crime scenes. After all, this was St. Louis and summer. All the druggers, domestic disputes, and crazies gave the cops plenty to do.

Carl was intrigued by the stack of notebooks, especially after he read snippets of the first couple of them, so he loaded them into the trunk of the Crown Vic. He would return them later, but first he had to notify the next of kin. This was the part of the job that he hated, especially when the victim was a kid. But even when it was an older person who died from an accident, the fact that the family had no warning that their relative was going to die made it much harder than the usual death from some medical problem.

After doing some searching, he found an address book in the old walnut desk in the small bedroom just off the living room. The desk looked like another Salvation Army leftover, or maybe some inexpensive pickup she got from one of those used furniture places over on Delmar. It was gouged, scarred, and well worn, but each drawer was neat and tidy, with stubs of the old Ticonderoga yellow pencils he used thirty years earlier. The erasers were those stick on types, because the original erasers on the stubs were long since worn away.

In the address book, he found the name Brian McCain, and a phone number, so he assumed that was a relative, probably the son whose pictures covered the wall. Carl was going to call the number, but he thought he would check out the son first, so he went out to the trunk of the Vic and found some of the journals that mentioned Brian.

Entry, December 1, 1972
I felt badly about not telling Miss Washington what had happened. I swallowed my pride and called her at the school and told her what happened, that I had to drop out to take care of my baby. She didn't ask me about how I got pregnant, and I didn't tell her because I didn't want her to think that it was my fault, like I asked for it or something.

She begged me to come back to school and said she would get Social Services or some other agency to help me and Brian, my baby, but I told her I couldn't. I told her I just wanted her to know that I was OK.

CHAPTER THREE

The drive to Fort Leonard Wood didn't take long at all. Carl decided it would be better to talk with the son face to face, rather than on the phone, and Carl lived out in the County anyway, so it wouldn't be that far out of his way. He dropped Mouse off at the office, since there was no need for both of them to go, and Mouse was dead serious about running by the house for a quickie.

Fort Leonard Wood is an army base about halfway between St. Louis and Springfield, Missouri. It is the U.S. Army Center for Chemical Corps and the training site for the Army Military Police Corps.

Carl checked in at Headquarters.

"I need to see one of your soldiers. A Captain Brian McCain," he explained to the corporal at the front desk.

"Who wants to see him and what about?" the corporal asked, without looking up from his computer.

Carl pulled out his badge and his credentials. "I'm from the State Police, and this is a personal matter."

"What kind of personal matter? Captain McCain is pretty busy right now."

Carl leaned over, got 6 inches from the soldier's face, and said, "Look at me. A personal matter means a personal matter and it's none of your goddamn business. And I'm pretty busy, too, so just get me Captain McCain right now and spare yourself a lot of misery down the way. Understand?"

The corporal obviously got the message real quickly. "I'll get him right away."

Five or ten minutes later, the guy in the pictures on the wall came out of an office and walked up to Carl.

"You got Corporal Rollins pretty shook up. I hope this is important."

"Yea, it's important. Is there somewhere we can talk?"

"I'm pretty busy right now," Brian said.

"For Christ sake, Captain," Carl said, with sarcastic emphasis on the "Captain" part. "Is everyone in the military this up tight? I need to talk to you, and I certainly am not here for my health, so just back off and at least hear what I have to say."

For what seemed like forever, the two men just looked at each other, two alpha males each staking out his territory. After 30 seconds or so, Brian said, "Sure, come on into my office."

They went into the office from which the captain had come. Carl quickly looked around. The office was what he thought would be a typical uptight military officer's seat of power—neat and organized, with everything in its place. Even the papers on the desk were stacked in piles with the edges all precisely arranged, certainly a far cry from Carl's desk at the station, which always looked like a tornado had just passed through.

The only personal item in the office was a single picture on the desk showing the handsome young man sitting behind the desk and a younger version of the lady Carl had just left an hour or so before.

"That is a very nice picture," Carl said. "I assume that is your mother."

"Yes, that is my mother, but I'm sure you didn't come all the way out here to the middle of nowhere to talk about my mother."

"Actually, I did," Carl said quietly. "I'm afraid there has been an accident at your mother's home, and she has died. I'm very sorry for your loss. Of course, I will need you to come in and make a formal identification, but it clearly is the same person as in the picture."

Brian had a blank faraway stare, but if Carl hadn't been looking for it, he never would have noticed because it lasted only a matter of seconds. The military training immediately took over, and Brian was back in control.

"What happened?"

"It looks like she was climbing on a chair to change a light bulb and the chair tipped over. We think her head hit the corner of the coffee table, but the ME will confirm that. When did you last see or speak with your mother?"

"I talked to her on the phone four days ago, and I was planning on driving over to see her next weekend. It would have been her birthday. When did the accident happen?"

"We're not sure, but I think she probably died about three days ago, based on the mail which was left in the box.

"Is there anyone you would like me to notify?" Carl asked.

"No, it was just me and my mother."

After a bit more conversation, they made arrangements for Brian to come in to do the formal identification, and Carl left, thinking that was the last he would ever see of Brian McCain, but that was not to be the case.

CHAPTER FOUR

A couple of days later, Carl was reviewing fitness reports for the squad. He hated the administrative duties and would much rather be out chasing the bad guys, but the paperwork was why he got the big bucks, he rationalized.

He barely heard the phone on his desk amidst the racket in the squad room. He glanced at the caller ID. The 573 area code faintly registered, as did the rest of the number, but he couldn't quite place it.

"Watson here."

"Lieutenant Watson, please hold for Captain McCain." Carl recognized the voice as the pain-in-the-ass corporal from Fort Leonard Wood. He wondered what Brian McCain wanted with him.

"Lieutenant, this is Brian McCain from Fort Leonard Wood."

"Yes, Captain, how may I help you?"

"I wondered if you would be able to come down here tomorrow. The Medical Examiner has completed the autopsy and has released my mother's body. The funeral is at 10 o'clock in the morning at the McNary Funeral Chapel, and I would like to meet with you for a few minutes afterwards. I may need your help on something."

"Can you give me some idea what this is about?"

"I'd rather discuss it personally, if you don't mind," Brian said. "I hope it isn't too much of an imposition, but it really is rather important."

"Sure, I can make it tomorrow," Carl said. He had originally planned on returning the journals he had retrieved from Missy McCain's home, but he had become intrigued by the few parts he had read, so he decided to not mention the journal, especially since it was apparent that Brian McCain was unaware that he had a sibling who was left at the hospital after birth or that his mother had written a journal.

"OK, I'll see you tomorrow," Brian responded.

Carl went looking for Mouse and found him digging into probably his third glazed doughnut of the morning, and it wasn't even 9:00 o'clock yet. The guy must have the metabolism of a hummingbird, Carl thought. He eats crap all day long and never gains a pound.

"Mouse, we are going down to Leonard Wood tomorrow," and he explained about the phone call.

"What in the hell could this be all about?" Mouse asked.

"Got me. We'll find out soon enough."

Carl dug out the journals he had retrieved from Missy McCain's home. He wasn't sure why he toted them off, but when he had read some of the early entries when he was at the scene, it roused his curiosity. He took the stack of notebooks to the copy room and made copies of them.

He had screwed around and stalled as much as he could. Back to the fitness reports.

CHAPTER FIVE

McNary's Funeral Home was just like any other, somber and poorly lit, with depressing music and hushed voices. "People talk about Celebration of Life," Mouse muttered to Carl, " but that is just a bunch of undertaker bullshit. If you really want to celebrate at a funeral, it should be like an Irish wake, with plenty of banter and booze. McNary sure must not be Irish, if there even is anyone named McNary still around."

Carl and Mouse saw Captain McCain across the room. He quickly came over to them.

"Captain, this is Sergeant Brannon, my partner. Mouse, this is Captain McCain, Ms. McCain's son."

"Nice to meet you, Sergeant. I appreciate both of you coming. After the service, maybe we can meet in the visitation room for a few minutes."

"Sure," Carl said, still wondering what the hell was going on here.

He and Mouse stood off to the side and watched the people. That's what cops do, they mostly watch people.

It was obvious that Captain McCain was well respected. There were lots of people there, and they seemed genuinely sorry for his loss. At lots of funerals, Carl thought, people come through the line like robots, with the standard impersonal utterances. This was different. The line dragged on pretty slowly because the people really seemed to have true empathy for Brian.

After the services, Brian brought some people over to meet Carl and Mouse.

"Lieutenant, Sergeant, this is Major General Frank Newton, the commanding officer here at Fort Leonard Wood, and these are his daughters, Lori and Kaitlyn."

"Nice to meet you," Carl and Mouse replied, almost in tandem.

The two daughters were spitting images of each other, obviously identical twins. It didn't take long, however, for both Carl and Mouse to see that they may have been identical, but they sure weren't the same.

Kaitlyn was very attentive to her father and equally supportive and empathetic toward Brian. She was very pretty, in an understated way, and conservatively dressed in a dark skirt and jacket with a pale blue blouse buttoned nearly to the top. She had on just a touch of makeup, and her hair was pulled back into a ponytail that made her look like a college coed, although

Carl figured she had to be at least in her late 20's or early 30's.

Lori, on the other hand, was constantly on the lookout, for what, Carl didn't know, but he suspected she was looking for her next conquest. Most of her attention seemed to be toward Brian. She made a point of coming over to him and hugging him. This was followed by a kiss that was more than a little inappropriate under the circumstance. Brian looked genuinely embarrassed and put off by her display.

In contrast to her sister, Lori was anything but conservative. She had on a shimmering dress which ended mid-thigh. It was tightly cut and showed off her more than ample figure to great advantage. In contrast to her more demure twin, Lori had obviously undergone breast augmentation. Although he tried not to notice, Carl couldn't help but focus on the swell of her supplemented breasts rising above the deeply cut neckline. She had oversized Oakley sunglasses perched atop her long blonde hair. All Carl could think was that she should have worn the sunglasses instead, since her eyes were red rimmed and dilated, not from crying, Carl was sure, but more likely from nose candy, he suspected. The swollen nasal mucosa and runny nose were just like Carl saw every day on the streets, signs of too much and too frequent cocaine.

After the perfunctory small talk, Brian ushered Carl and Mouse into a back room at the funeral home.

"Lieutenant, I think I may need your help," Brian started.

"How so?"

"What did you think of the Newtons?" Brian asked.

"What do you mean, what did I think?"

"You know, any first impressions?" Brian responded.

Mouse quickly interjected, "I'll answer that. The Major General obviously has great respect for you, but I sense it is something more than just professional respect. The cute girl, Kaitlyn, feels the same way as her father. The other one, Lori, is street savvy, manipulative, wants to get into your pants, if she hasn't already, and is a regular drug user. I wouldn't trust her as far as I can throw her. Not only that, she was sizing you up, Carl, to see if maybe she could take both of you guys on."

The door opened without any warning and the asshole corporal entered.

"Oh, I'm sorry to interrupt. I didn't realize anyone was in here."

"We are busy, Corporal Rollins."

"Yes, sir. Anything I can do to help?"

"No. We are discussing some personal issues, Corporal. You are excused."

Carl turned to Mouse. "You are full of shit. That Lori clearly is different from her sister, but there is no way she was making a move on me."

Brian smiled. "Sergeant, you are very perceptive. The reason I asked your first impression is because there is something going on her at the base, and I want to get to the bottom of it, but I don't want it to have collateral damage, if you know what I mean."

Carl and Mouse both waited patiently for Brian to continue.

"I think it would be best if I go back to the beginning."

CHAPTER SIX

"You have to understand," Brian started. "My mother came from nothing. She was an intelligent, but uneducated, single black 16-year-old mother with a newborn infant, no money, no future, and no one to turn to. By the grace of God, one of her teachers took a liking to my mother. Fortunately for us, Miss Washington, the teacher, had a brother who ran the office for the commanding officer here at Fort Leonard Wood at the time. The Major General needed a maid, so my mama and I moved here. At least we now had a roof over our head and food to eat. After five years or so, Major General Newton was reassigned as the new commandant, and my mother was kept on as his housekeeper and maid.

"Then the General's wife died two years later of metastatic breast cancer, so the General was left caring for his twin daughters, four-year-old army brats who had never lived in one place for more than two years at a time. My mother now became the nanny and surrogate mother for the two of them, at the same time raising me.

"Over the years, it was obvious to my mama that Lori was an independent spirit, always pushing to the limit of everything she did, academically, socially, morally, everything. You can argue about nature versus nurture, but these two twins didn't fit any of the molds. They had the same genes, the same homes, and the same opportunities, but they were as different as they could possibly be.

"The good thing that happened," Brian continued, "was that the general took a liking to me. It was almost as though I was going to substitute for the daughter that he had essentially lost. Not only that, he assumed the role of my substitute father in exchange for my mother taking on the responsibility of substitute mother for his daughters. During all this time, Kaitlyn was the lost soul. Lori and I got the attention, me for my successes on the athletic field and in the classroom, and Lori for all of her failures and indiscretions. Kaitlyn, though, is much stronger than you might suspect, so she blossomed over the years, despite being shuffled to the side."

Carl interjected, "I noticed some photographs at your mother's house in which you were graduating from somewhere. From the uniforms, it looked like West Point."

"That's right," Brian responded. "The General pulled some strings and got me appointed, and I graduated third in my class. After that, I went through Ranger training and spent time in the Middle East. I had some injuries while in Afghanistan, so I was reassigned here."

"You were shot?" Mouse asked.

"Yeah, a couple of times, but the medics kept me going until the docs put me back together, so I'm pretty much okay now.

"The reason I wanted you to know all this is because I have a real affection for Major General Newton. He has turned my life around and helped turn my mother's life around, so I don't want anything bad to happen to him, you know what I mean?"

"What bad might happen?" Carl asked.

Brian continued, "Army life can be like police life, ninety percent of the time it is boring as hell, and the other ten percent is an adrenaline rush beyond description. Many of the soldiers can't deal with the emotional ups and downs, so they end up on booze or drugs or both. Every army base has that problem, but we just may have it worse than some.

"Lieutenant, we have a real drug problem here at Leonard Wood. There has to be someone on base who is the supplier. There are just too many users for them to get their supplies randomly on the street. We need to find out the source of the drugs and cut off the supply, and to do that, I need your help. I don't want any of this to reflect poorly on the General's command, you know what I mean? That's what I meant earlier by collateral damage."

Mouse spoke up. "Why do you need us? This is the Army training center for the Military Police. Surely there is someone here who could investigate this."

"There is," Brian replied, "but they are concerned about their own careers, and I don't know that the fox isn't already in the hen house. The MP's may be willing to throw General Newton under the bus just to cover their own asses."

Carl was concerned about stepping on jurisdictional toes. "We would need to be asked in to investigate this. It sounds like a real can of worms that we really don't need."

"I've already cleared it with General Newton," Brian responded. "You will have full access and authority. Most importantly, you have resources off base that we don't have, and I think the drugs may be coming from St. Louis, so it really does make more sense for you to take over."

"All right," Carl said. "I'll think about it and get back to you."

As he was about to leave, Carl asked, "By the way, you told me earlier that there was just you and your mother. You have no brothers, sister, aunts, uncles, anyone?"

"No, just the two of us. Why do you ask?"

"I just wanted to make sure all the relatives had been contacted."

Carl and Mouse got up to leave. As they opened the door, Corporal Rollins was loitering nearby. The two cops looked at each other with an understanding brought on my years of working together. This guy is creepy and nosy, they thought.

As they got back into the car, Mouse took his usual spot riding shotgun.

Carl always shared everything with Mouse, but for some reason, his instinct told him to just keep quiet about the journal for a while. He decided to read some more of Missy McCain's journal as soon as he could find the time.

"That is one complicated family, don't you think, Mouse?"

"What do you mean?"

"Well, you've got a surrogate father for the captain; a surrogate mother for the twin girls, who happen to look identical, except for the plastic surgery, of course, but who are otherwise as different as night and day; a drug problem on the base; a general's daughter who obviously is into drugs; the sudden departure of the nanny/mother for unknown reasons, followed by her unexpected death."

"You don't really think Missy McCain's death was anything but an accident do you?"

"No, not really," Carl said, "but you know how I am. I just don't like any loose ends."

16

CHAPTER SEVEN

Because he wanted some time alone to read more of the McCain journal, Carl had dropped Mouse off at the office. Missy McCain's early entries had given him some ideas as to how to address some of the "loose ends" he and Mouse had discussed.

Entry, May 6, 1991

General Newton asked me about the twins. I have tried to make him understand that Lori is becoming more difficult now that she is getting older— running around with the "wrong crowd," skipping school, maybe into the drug scene. He seems at a loss as to how to deal with her. He thinks that it is just a teenage rebellious phase which she will outgrow. He is more concerned about Kate, the sensitive one, and he is afraid she will feel neglected. I told him that Kate will be fine. She is the stronger, more secure of the twins, and it is Kate who tries to keep Lori grounded as much as possible. I hope he hasn't given up on Lori. She needs him now more than ever.

Entry, September 11, 1993

Kate and Lori are like my own daughters. I have done the best I can to help fill the void after their mother died. The irony of it is that while I am helping raise someone else's children, I frequently think about the children I left behind. Brian has been a wonderful son, and I am grateful and blessed to have him, but it still wears heavily on me when I think of my other children. Despite the fact that I don't know them, I can't help but worry and wonder about them—that's what mothers do. Are they safe? Are they happy?

Carl leaned back in his chair and considered what he had just read. Just as in his own life, Missy McCain did what she felt she had to do, not just to protect Brian's future and her own future, but also to protect the future of the children she really didn't know. It was almost as though she realized that she would have to sacrifice part of her family to save all of them. Her only hope was that the children who had to be given up would be well cared for.

Carl's own mother must have gone through similar thought processes when she gave him up to the foster care system. He had been fortunate in that he was eventually placed with the Watsons, a loving and caring couple who loved him as their own, so much so that they formally adopted him when he was eight years old. He was sure that this gap in his life—the uncertainty of who he was and where his roots were—and the similarities between his life and that of Missy and Brian McCain were what made Carl become more compelled to delve into her background.

Entry, September 25, 2007

Lori Newton told her father that I was the one who has been taking his OxyContin. Of course I know his old injury flares up once in a while, but I have no need for his drugs, and one look at Lori makes it obvious that she is getting drugs from somewhere, probably from his medicine cabinet and on the street. The General says he believes me, but rather than create a problem for Brian or the General, it is better just to leave. "I hope you understand, Missy," the General told me. "I really have no choice but to agree that it would be better if you left, but don't worry, I will make sure you're taken care of."

Well, Carl though, now I have one "loose end" tied up—that explains why Missy moved off the base so unexpectedly.

CHAPTER EIGHT

Dewayne Foster loved his Chevy. This Chevy is hot and sexy, Dewayne thought to himself, but not nearly as hot and sexy as the owner. Nobody called Dewayne by his real name, at least they didn't do it twice. Most people didn't even know what his given name was. They just knew him as Faster Foster. And anybody on the street who called him Dewayne was told in no uncertain terms that his name was Faster. If they made the same mistake a second time, Faster's guys would beat the crap out of them.

Dewayne came up with the name Faster by himself, because his whole life, at least in his mind, was done at a faster pace than the rest of the world. He picked up women and went through them at a faster pace. His drug trade grew at a faster pace. Hell, he even talked faster than the rest of the world. Of course, that was because he usually was revved up by his drugs. After loving himself and his '57 Chevy most, Dewayne's next favorite was his nose candy.

The Chevy idled at the red light in the heart of Delmar, the center of St. Louis' black inner city. This was Dewayne's turf, and when he was out making the rounds on his distributors, the word would get out real fast—"Faster's out. Better shape up."

The unmarked car pulled up beside Faster at the light. Although it was unmarked, it was obviously the cops. They didn't care, though, if they were made. The two black cops just wanted to tweek Faster and yank his chain.

"Hey, Dewayne, bro'," the cop riding shotgun hollered through the window.

"My name is Faster, and you can call me Faster."

"Yeah," the cop responded. "Faster and Slower," making reference to the black dude riding with Faster. The second guy's real name was Rufus Stoker, but he picked up the moniker "Slower Stoker" mainly because he was the opposite of Faster, all muscle and real short in the smarts department. Even to his face, Faster referred to his bodyguard as Slower, but guys on the street didn't, unless they wanted to get smacked around by the overgrown ape. Guys on the street loved nicknames, and Faster and Slower just seemed to go together, so that was Slower's street name behind his back.

Dewayne drove around for a while, checking on his operation. He liked to think that he was like UPS or FedEx, a complex distribution company providing a service to the community. In reality, he did have a very efficient system for getting his product to the consumers, so to speak, but Faster was never satisfied. In fact, he was always looking to expand. That's what the meeting back at the loft later today was all about.

The Chevy was a beauty—candy apple red convertible, with white Naugahyde rolled and pleated interior, a Hearst transmission, and what they used to call an Okie-rake in the 50's. The back end springs were fixed so the tail end rose only about 4 inches above the pavement. With the front a lot higher than the back, Dewayne looked like he was always driving uphill, but he thought it made him look more important. The problem was that the Okie-rake made it impossible for Faster and Slower to take the Chevy out on the road when the snow came, but he had a couple of other cars he could take out then.

Dewayne dropped Slower off at what Dewayne liked to call the office. Actually, it was the back of an old warehouse which they had converted into a comfortable out- of-the- way place to conduct business. The best thing about it was that there was nothing much nearby, so they could always keep tabs on who was hanging around, especially since they had an intricate series of alarms and surveillance cameras, complete with monitors in the office.

Dewayne then proceeded downtown to his loft. This had been an abandoned factory, and when the alderman took it upon themselves to try to renovate the downtown area, Dewayne managed to purchase the building, using a dummy corporation, and developed it into several condominiums. There were two units on the lower floors, but Faster had the entire top floor for himself, complete with his own elevator and entry, separate security system, and private garage. He wasn't going to take any chances that the competition was going to surprise him.

Right at two o'clock, the guard downstairs called and told Faster that he had a visitor, the person that he was expecting. Faster told him to send her up, and he went over to the wet bar and mixed a couple of drinks. It was only two o'clock, but like Jimmy Buffett said, "It's five o'clock somewhere," and this babe likes her Coke and rum with her coke. Faster laughed at his wit," Coke and rum with her coke," pretty clever.

CHAPTER NINE

As Lori Newton rode up the mirrored elevator, she admired herself in the reflection.

"Not bad at all," she thought.

She was wearing a dress that reminded her of what her high school speech teacher had said about a good speech. "It should be long enough to cover the subject, but short enough to be interesting." The dress was barely long enough to cover the subject, but it certainly was short enough to be interesting.

Faster was waiting for her right outside the elevator door when it opened. He had a handgun at his side, but that didn't surprise Lori because he always had that gun ready whenever someone got off the elevator. He told her he didn't like to be surprised.

Faster stood back and admired the view as Lori pirouetted for him.

"I like it, I like it a lot, Snowflake," Faster admired.

"Why did you call me Snowflake?"

"I was just thinking," Faster replied. "You are blonde, pale as the driven snow, beautiful and unique, just like a snowflake."

"But you forgot, Dewayne, that there is something wrong with that analogy. There are no two snowflakes alike, and I have an identical twin."

"Baby, from what you told me, you and your sister may look alike, but you are anything but identical, believe me. The two of you are as different as the two of us."

Lori thought about that for a minute. Dewayne probably was right. She and her sister were very different, and there was no doubt that she and Dewayne were very different, at least physically.

Dewayne was about 6 feet tall, but the drugs had taken their toll over the years. He was thin and emaciated, but he still worked out so what muscles he still did have were pretty well defined. Not at all like Brian McCain, by any means. Brian was a real hunk. Now there was a guy that she would love to get into the sack. Maybe some day.

Meanwhile, Lori's thoughts came back to Dewayne. He had a full beard and for some reason had reverted to the old Afro hair style from the 60's. Somehow, though, he could pull it off, and the style really didn't look bad at all on him.

The two of them went into the condo. The inside certainly looked nothing like the exterior of the building. Although Faster had spent a lot of money to help gentrify the building, the exterior looked like an aging Hollywood actress who had one too many plastic surgeons put his kids through college on her ticket. Inside, though, the living room was large and completely done in white. It had modern glass and steel furniture, upholstered in white, with oyster shell white walls and ceilings, decorated with modernistic paintings, which Lori knew were not inexpensive reproductions.

The kitchen was also state of the art, with granite counter tops and large stainless steel appliances. In fact, Dewayne fancied himself a pretty good cook, and the kitchen rivaled what you could find in an upscale restaurant.

"I fixed you a rum and Coke. That's your beverage of choice, right, Snowflake?"

"Yeah, that's what I want, but I don't like it when you call me Snowflake."

"I don't know why not. You know, it's just my special name for my special girl."

"Cut the crap, Dewayne. I'm not your special girl. You've got girls stashed all over St. Louis, and probably in six other states. You and I are business partners and fucking partners, and nothing else. This is a diversion for us and takes care of our needs, because we both know we are just a couple of horny bastards."

"I'll tell you what, Snowflake. I'll stop calling you Snowflake if you stop calling me Dewayne. You know I go by Faster."

"No deal. I hate that name. Besides," Lori said, as she brought out her most seductive, sexy voice, "I like it slower, not faster, so we'll just keep it as it is." With that, she reached down, rubbed his crotch, and said, "How about a little nose dust and a slow roll in that big playpen in your bedroom?"

An hour later, the two of them were spent as they lay entwined among the disheveled bed clothes. They looked like a big Oreo cookie, with Faster's jet black legs wrapped around Lori's lily white thighs.

"Why do you get your rocks off with a downtown brother, Snowflake? Surely there's lots of prime cock with all those horny guys out at the base."

"Why, Dewayne, are you insecure?" she asked tauntingly.

"I told you not to call me that," he interrupted.

"Sure, Faster," Lori said, facetiously putting emphasis on his street name.

22

"Do you remember the movie, *Blazing Saddles*?" she asked.

"Yeah, the one with Madeline Kahn and Cleavon Little—a real comedy classic."

"Remember what she said to Cleavon, when she asked, 'Is it true what they say about black men?' And she then unzipped his pants and said, 'It's true, it's true.' That's why I like fucking you, Faster, because it's true, it's true. Not only that. Admit it, we are two people who like sex way too much, especially without any strings attached."

CHAPTER TEN

Carl dropped Mouse off at the office and headed to the County Clerk's office. One of his old high school classmates, Susan Billingsley, ran the office, although the Chief Clerk thought he did.

After he parked the Crown Vic in the "Reserved" space, he flipped down the visor with the Detective Division card on it, and entered the building. The County Clerk's office was on the second floor.

"Hey, Susan, long time, no see."

"That's not my fault, Carl. You know where to find me. Of course, the only time you call is when you want something," she said with that sassy smile on her face.

Susan was a very attractive African American whom Carl had dated briefly in high school. She married shortly after graduation, and her husband of nearly 18 years was now a St. Louis City policeman. She and Carl enjoyed the banter back and forth whenever they saw each other, which wasn't very often.

"What favor does my second favorite upholder of truth, justice, and the American way need today?" Susan asked.

"Susan, I'm working on a case and I need some birth records from the old City Hospital from 1972. When was it that the City closed, and where would the records be now?"

Susan looked it up on the computer. "City Hospital closed in 1985. All the records are in storage in the Public Works warehouse way over on Essex Street. You know where that is?"

"Yeah, I know," Carl responded. "Do you think they will still have records from over thirty years ago?"

"I don't know whether they will have them, and if they do, I don't know whether there is any way for you to figure out which box they are in. They didn't have computers way back then, so you'll just have to sort through lots of paper to find out."

"Thanks, Susan. I owe you."

"Carl, you have owed me for years, and some day I may try and collect. Maybe you'll let me fix you up with one of my girlfriends some time. That would pay off the debt."

"Thanks for the offer, Susan, but I think I'll pass for now."

Carl turned and left as Susan smiled and quietly shook her head. Some girl is really missing out, she thought.

Carl drove over to the warehouse on Essex. It was a two story cinder block building probably built with federal funds after World War II. An institutional parking lot sprouted tufts of sun- bleached weeds through the cracked asphalt. Obviously, no money was spent for landscaping. The building was aged and depressing.

Inside, Carl was directed to an office on the second floor. He found the employees to be exactly like the building in which they worked 8 hours a day, aged and depressing. Carl figured most of them worked somewhere else in the public sector years ago but had been reassigned here to be "put out to pasture." They were universally sour, uninterested, and not at all anxious to help the public, or even the police, for that matter.

Carl told the worker in the "Files" section what he wanted. He was told that all the City Hospital records were in a storage cubicle in the basement, but over the years, many files had been lost or damaged during water breaks, moves, and even one fire. Carl wasn't particularly optimistic that he would be able to find what he was after, but he decided to give it a try.

The basement was dusty, moldy, and poorly lit. Carl went back to the "cage" where he had been told the records from the City Hospital were supposed to be. There were rows and rows of bankers' boxes stacked 6 high, over 400 of them total. Carl went up and down the rows until he found a box labeled "1/72-6/72, OB," which he assumed contained the obstetric records from June of '72.

He spent 45 minutes going through dusty papers, many of which were illegible, either because the ink was so faded, the light was so poor, or, mostly because the doctors and nurses handwriting was so bad that even the CIA couldn't interpret it. Finally, he found what he was looking for.

Carl broke out into a sweat, and he could feel his heart rate pick up. He figured it was because the air down in the basement was so stifling and wasn't moving at all. He carefully read the papers in his hand, smiled, and thought aloud, "Another loose end tied up. Very interesting." He carefully folded the documents and put them into his inner coat pocket.

CHAPTER ELEVEN

Carl returned to the office to pick up Mouse and they drove into St. Louis to touch base with the St. Louis City Police Narcotics Squad. If Captain McCain suspected that the drugs at Fort Leonard Wood were coming from the city, it seemed like a good idea to start with the guys who would know who the players were.

"Hey, Fogarty," Mouse greeted the big ruddy faced Irishman.

"Oh, shit, this can't be good. What in the hell do you want, Mouse? Every time I see your ugly puss, it turns into a day from hell."

"Happy to see you, too, Fogarty," Mouse smiled.

"Carl, this is Cornelius Fogarty, narc extraordinaire. Con, this is Carl Watson, my partner. Carl, Con has been a narcotics cop for as long as I can remember. He knows more about what's going on in the drug trade in St. Louis than the pushers themselves know. In fact, are you on your second or your third generation of drug dealers, Con?"

"Nice to meet you, Con. What we need is some information. Mouse and I have been asked to look into the drug trade out at Leonard Wood, and we thought that it would be a good idea to start here in the city, since we think this is where the trafficking is probably originating. Can you fill us in on who the players are?"

"Sure, Lieutenant, be happy to."

"Please, cut the formalities. Just call me Carl."

"Okay, Carl."

"There are quite a few small fish in the pond," Fogarty began. "You know, little guys who have delusions of grandeur. They see big dollars, big cars, big girls with big tits, you know what I mean? But these small operators would be way out of their league trying to peddle drugs at Leonard Wood. There are only a couple of locals who have the distribution system to take on a new territory of that size, and the only one who seems to be in expansion mode, you know, is Dewayne Foster.

"Dewayne goes by Faster—Faster Foster, get it," Fogarty continued. "Jesus Christ, these guys all think they have to have a moniker, you know. You know what his dumb-ass sidekick's name is? Rufus Stoker. And you know what his street name is? Slower. Faster Foster and Slower Stoker, like

Tweedle-dee and Tweedle-dum; more like Tweedle-Dumb and Tweedle-Dumber.

"Anyway, Foster actually has put together a pretty efficient operation. We have had our eye on him for quite a while, and we are trying to put together a case, but, you know, these things take time. But I think he is the most likely brains behind what you are looking for, although I feel stupid myself using brains and Faster Foster in the same sentence.'

"What's the best way to get to Foster?" Carl asked. "I'm thinking about just taking the direct approach and trying to size him up, but I don't want to step on your toes or get in the way of your investigation. Any thoughts?"

"Carl, Faster knows we are looking at him, but he is either so dumb or so clever that he doesn't seem to mind. So far, we don't have any hard evidence, so we'll just keep on yanking his chain until he screws up, which he certainly will do somewhere along the line. I'd be happy to introduce you to him. In fact, I'll just stand in the background and see how he reacts when he finds out that the State cops are now looking at him."

"Sounds like a plan, Con. Let's set it up."

CHAPTER TWELVE

Carl and Mouse drove Fogarty over to Foster's hideaway. Outside the private entry, they were confronted by a goon who looked like he may have been on the losing side of a St. Louis Rams practice game, muscular and tattooed and with a nose that had seen more than its share of forearm shivers or fists.

"What's the fuzz want?" he asked.

Con replied, "We're here to pay a social call on Faster. You know, to see if he is available to attend the annual Policeman's Ball."

"Cut the crap, Fogarty," the behemoth responded. "Mr. Foster is busy."

"The only time Faster is busy is when he's jacking off in the bathroom, and then it's just because he can't handle the tweezers and pecker at the same time," Fogarty shot back.

Carl intervened. "OK, guys, enough of the locker room banter. We would like to speak with Foster about business, so just call upstairs and tell him we are coming up."

The bodyguard gave Carl a curious look and went over to the phone hanging just inside the exterior door. "Faster, Fogarty and a couple of cops I don't recognize are down here, and they say they want to talk with you."

The goon awaited the answer, then hung up and said, "Faster said to go on up."

Faster met the trio at the elevator, but this time, he left his handgun inside.

"Well, hello Sergeant Fogarty, how nice to see you again," Faster facetiously remarked. "Who are your babysitters?"

"Can it, Faster. This is Lieutenant Watson and Sergeant Brannon from the State Police. They have a couple of questions they want to ask you."

The foursome entered Faster's condo.

"Nice place," Mouse observed. "The drug trade must pay well."

"I wouldn't know, Sergeant. My import and export business pays quite well and has allowed me to achieve a very comfortable life," Faster sarcastically responded with a grin.

Carl eyed the gaunt black man carefully as Faster and Mouse continued their repartee. Foster had multiple bruises on the arms, which were difficult to see under the darkly pigmented skin, but the most noticeable thing was the constant drip of fresh blood from the drugger'snose. Carl assumed that was a result of chronic cocaine use, but it certainly was more than he usually saw.

"Mr. Foster, I've got to take a leak," Carl said. "You got a john in this place?"

"Yeah. It's right down that hall," and Faster pointed off to the left.

Carl found the rest room, went in, and relieved himself. While there, he looked around. He saw a wad of bloody Kleenex tissues and a couple of used Trojans in the waste can.

I wonder who the lucky girl was, Carl mused

Mouse was quizzing Faster. "We're looking into a drug problem out at Fort Leonard Wood," Mouse said. "You wouldn't happen to have any information about that, would you?"

"Why would I know anything about drugs or Fort Leonard Wood?" Faster asked. "Those guys don't have much disposable income to purchase things from my import/export inventory."

Fogarty couldn't keep still a minute longer. "Faster, the only imports you get are from Colombia via Mexico, and the only exports are dead bodies you ship back "

"Why, Fogarty, I have no idea what you are talking about."

Mouse became more assertive and got right in Faster's face. "Listen, asshole, we know you are no more in the import/export business than I am. Not only that, we know you are a player in the drug scene, so we want some straight answers, and we want them now. What do you know about drugs getting out to Fort Leonard Wood?"

Faster was becoming more agitated now, so he dropped his sarcastic demeanor and stared at Mouse as he replied, "I know nothing about drugs at Fort Leonard Wood, the Pentagon, St. Louis, or anywhere else, so, if you have any more questions, you can talk to my attorney. Now get your asses out of my condo."

It was obvious that they weren't going to get any useful information from Faster, so the three cops left.

As they got into the car, Fogarty said, "Well, that was a waste of time."

"I'm not so sure," Carl replied. "He seemed to get a little jittery when Mouse brought up Leonard Wood. I think he knows a lot more about what's going on out there than he's letting on. What did you expect, Con, that he

would just open up and spill his guts to us? We need to keep putting
the pressure on him. It would help if you could have a couple of your guys
keep their eyes on him for a while. They might give us a lead where to look
next."

"I'll get right on it," Fogarty responded.

CHAPTER THIRTEEN

After the cops left, Faster called Slower Stoker.

"Get your ass over here, Slower. We may have a problem."

Twenty minutes later, Slower walked into the penthouse. "What's the deal," he said.

"The cops are poking around, that's what the deal is. We need to keep our eyes and ears open, because they're looking into our operation out at the base."

"How do you think they heard about that?"

"I have no idea, but I'm worried that that ditzy blonde may be shooting her mouth off. You know how she gets when she's had a snort or two. She can't keep her clothes on or her mouth shut. God only knows what she's saying when she rolling around in the hay with a whole platoon of soldiers. I need to talk to her. Get a hold of her, Slower, and tell her to get her tight little white ass over here. And I mean now."

"I'll take care of it right away, boss."

After Slower took off to contact Lori Newton, Faster went into the bathroom. His nose had started bleeding even more. He took a bunch of toilet paper and made it into a makeshift packing and shoved the wad up into both sides of his nose. When he looked into the mirror, he also noticed that his gums looked all swollen, and they were oozing bright red blood also. Faster had bleeding from the nose for a long time, and he always attributed it to his cocaine, but it was much more frequent in the last couple of weeks, and the oozing was harder to stop now than it had been. He also had noticed that he was bruising easier than he used to.

"I may need to go see the doc one of these days," he said to his reflection, "but he will just tell me to lay off the candy for awhile. I'll just cool it with the snorting and see if it gets better."

CHAPTER FOURTEEN

It took two days for Fogarty to get approval for surveillance of Foster's condo. Although he couldn't commit to round the clock observation, Fogarty promised to get some eyes out there, and he commissioned overtime to monitor Faster's visitors and activities as much as possible. Fogarty agreed with Carl and Mouse that Faster may be the key to a much larger operation than the city cops originally suspected.

Carl drove over to the County Crime Lab. He had some off the record testing that he needed done. He strolled into the lab and crossed over to a large workbench complete with all kinds of expensive looking instruments. He walked up to an emaciated middle- aged lab tech wearing a starched brilliant white coat and Coke-bottle glasses so thick that they made his pupils look like something from a cartoon doll.

"Hey, Arnold, how ya' doing?"

The pale lab tech was so preoccupied with his work he nearly jumped out of his Hush Puppies.

"Jeez, Carl, you scared me. I didn't hear you come in."

"Sorry, Arnold, I didn't mean to startle you. Listen, I have a question. Is it possible to compare the footprint that shows up on a newborn's birth certificate from 30 years age to a current toe print to see if there is a match?"

"Sure, we could do that, but only if the original footprint had some pretty good images of the toe, rather than just the soles of the feet, and if the adult print is from a toe that is not too calloused. Is this a case you are working on?"

"Yeah, it's early in a case, so I really don't need a formal report, but I just need the information to help direct me which way to go."

Carl reached into his jacket pocket and removed a glassine envelope with a paper in it and another document which looked pretty official. The document had an infant footprint on it. He handed both to the lab tech.

As he pointed at the glassine envelope, Arnold asked, "What's this?"

"That's the toe print on a piece of paper and the other is the footprint. I need to know whether they belong to the same person."

The tech looked carefully at the birth certificate. "I think there is enough definition of the loops and whorls from the toes that I can give you a pretty good idea whether there is a match, but it certainly won't be definitive enough for me to swear to in court without more study."

"All I need is an off the cuff best guess."

Foregoing all the fancy, expensive equipment, Arnold reached into a desk drawer and took out an old fashioned magnifying glass. "Probably made by the same company that supplied Sherlock Holmes," Carl thought.

After 5 minutes or so, the tech looked up. "I can't be absolutely sure, Carl, but I would bet you an awful lot of money that these two prints came from the same person."

"Bingo," Carl said, a large grin on his face. "That helps a lot. You can just forget that we had this conversation, Arnold, since I really didn't get the samples in the usual fashion. If I need a formal statement, I'll follow procedure and get back to you. I really appreciate it."

Most of the cops treated Arnold like he was an insignificant lab animal, just like the white mice he still used, but Carl always thanked him and seemed truly appreciative of his work. That's why he grinned almost as broadly as Carl did when he got the match.

"Any time, Carl, and don't worry. I'll keep this under my hat."

Carl left the lab and walked to his car, not realizing that he was whistling a happy tune as he did so.

CHAPTER FIFTEEN

Surveillance duty is the bane of a cop's existence. It is hours of boredom interspersed rarely with a few minutes of euphoria if they were lucky enough to see anything of interest. The worst thing, other than the boredom and the body odor which accumulated while two overweight middle-aged grunts with too much testosterone and too many cigarettes sat in a beat up police car with worn out seat springs and no air conditioning during a St. Louis summer, was the fact that they always seemed to have to take a leak or pass gas. So they pissed in an empty plastic Coke bottle and farted, not particularly conducive to an ideal work environment. Once in a while, though, they had to get out and stretch.

The cops that Fogarty sent out to keep an eye on Faster were ticked off from the get-go, just because they didn't want to be there. It was even worse because they really didn't think they would learn anything useful, at least not without wasting many hours watching a derelict old former factory.

Much to their surprise, they had only been sitting in their unmarked car, unobtrusive amongst a queue of decrepit cars parked up and down the filthy street, for only a couple of hours when a fancy BMW came whipping around the corner and slid to a stop just in front of Faster's building.

"That's a nice set of wheels," the patrolman said to his partner.

"That it is. I'm sure they don't see a lot of Beemer convertibles in this part of town."

The cops then really took notice when a sexy, sensuous blond wormed her way out of the low slung driver's seat. Her skirt was so short that they both got an eyeful of a tanned and finely tuned thigh.

"Holy shit. The set of wheels on the car was nice, but look at the set of wheels on that babe. I wonder what the hell she is doing down here in nigger town."

'Good question," his partner responded, his eyes almost falling out of their orbits. "You may be a leg man, but I am a tit man. Look at the set of knockers on her. I could bury my face in those for hours, and if I suffocated, what a great way to go."

As soon as the cops noticed that she was headed towards Faster's building with a very purposeful stride, they quickly came back to reality.

"You take some pictures of the broad and I'll phone in the plate numbers to get a make on the car."

"Okay, Sarge," and the patrolman directed the viewfinder on the camera toward the door to the building and snapped a series of photos. It was obvious that the foxy visitor was no stranger to the bodyguard at the door, since he greeted her with a familiarity that indicated she was more than a casual acquaintance.

The patrolman then took some pictures of the license plate and the car. He also noted a parking decal on the lower driver's side on the front windshield. Using the zoom, he could read the lettering and took some more photos..

"The parking sticker says Fort Leonard Wood," he mumbled to his sergeant. " I wonder who she is."

The sergeant held up his finger to silence his partner as he listened on his cell phone.

"General Frank Newton. Got it," and he hung up.

"The car is registered to a General Frank Newton, whose address is on base housing at Leonard Wood. Central ran a quick Google search on him and found out that he is the Commanding Officer. That must be either his very young wife, his very young girlfriend, or his daughter."

The girl went into the building and stayed inside for a half hour or so. When she exited, she was in a far different frame of mind than when she entered. She was pissed. Her face was bright red and she turned around and got nose to nose with the black dude who had followed her out to the street. The cops recognized the guy as Faster Foster, so they watched the scene unfold and continued to take photos.

The two of them were obviously having more than a minor disagreement. Faster grabbed the blonde by the arm and spun her around. He hollered loud enough that the two cops could hear him very clearly.

"Listen, Lori, we need to back off for a while. The cops are all over me like stink on shit. It's too dangerous to push more stuff on base, at least for now."

The blonde got in his face. "You listen, you ball-less asshole. I've got people expecting us to come through, and these aren't very nice people. If you can't supply what I need, I'll find someone who will. You're not the only fish in the sea. I can think of two guys right off the top of my head who would be more than happy to pick up after you, you gutless prick." With that she jumped into her BMW and sped off, her rear tires flipping up garbage and filthy gutter water right into Faster's face.

Faster turned to Slower. "We're going to have to do something with that drugged up bitch. She's a loose cannon who is going to take us down with her when she crashes."

The cops looked at each other as though they had just won the lottery.

"Holy shit," the sergeant said to no one in particular. "Fogarty and those hot-shit State Cops are going to owe us big time."

CHAPTER SIXTEEN

After hearing from the cops watching Faster, Fogarty got in touch with Carl and Mouse and all five of them met at Fogarty'office.

"Are you guys sure that the blonde and Faster are in cahoots?" Carl asked.

They both nodded. "I can tell you, Lieutenant, that those two are in business together, but they are totally pissed at each other. You and Fogarty obviously shook Foster up big time, but the girl doesn't want to hear about it. All she cares about is her drug business and keeping the flow going."

"Sarge is right, Lieutenant. Those two are supplying the drugs to Fort Leonard Wood, and she has no intention of slowing down the trade just because you guys are watching. She must be either really stupid or really greedy because it's obvious she's not going to give it up."

"Thanks for the great work, guys," Fogarty told them. "Even though we know who's behind the drug flow, knowing it and proving it are two different things, so I need you to go on home and get some sleep. The Lieutenant, Mouse and I will work on the girl."

The two cops left, and Carl then said to Fogarty, "I think we need to let Captain McCain at the base know what's going down, since he was the one who invited us in to begin with. I don't envy him one bit. Remember how he wanted to avoid what he called 'collateral damage' with this operation? With the General's daughter a major player in this deal, there is going to be much more than collateral damage. This is going to be a tsunami as far as McCain is concerned."

Carl then called Brian McCain at his office. His corporal answered, "Captain McCain's office."

"Corporal, this is Lieutenant Watson. Is Captain McCain available?"

"May I ask what this is concerning?"

"Corporal, we are not playing that game again. No, you may not ask what this is concerning. Just put Captain McCain on the line."

Brian came on the line quickly thereafter. "Hello, Lieutenant. How may I help you?"

"Please, call me Carl, Captain, and we have some new information about the situation we have been looking into for you. I would like to meet with you and fill you in."

"I go by Brian, by the way. You really made fast work. What have you learned?"

Carl sensed quiet breathing on the connection. "I think it would be best if we drove down there to bring you up to date. Are you free around two this afternoon?"

"Two would be fine, Carl. I will see you then."

Brian hung up, and Carl waited just a second before he disconnected. He heard a separate click on the other end of the line, smiled, and then put the handset into its cradle.

CHAPTER SEVENTEEN

Entry, June 20, 2008

I don't know what to do. What will General Newton believe if I tell him that I have proof that Lori is selling drugs on base? Will he think I am just being vindictive and take it out on Brian? I can't take that chance. Maybe I should just talk with Lori and tell her what I know. Maybe she will stop.

This was the last entry that Carl Watson found in Missy McCain's journal. He wondered what the "proof" was. He went back and reviewed previous entries and found no clue as to what Missy McCain had found to substantiate that Lori Newton was involved with the drug trade on the base. He also wondered how Lori, as volatile as she was, would have reacted, particularly if she felt threatened by Missy.

CHAPTER EIGHTEEN

The three of them piled into the Crown Vic, Carl driving and Mouse riding shotgun, as usual, with Fogarty in the back seat.

"How are we going to deal with McCain, Carl," Mouse asked.

"I think he is an upright guy, and he deserves the truth. He can deal with it. Not only that, when this all crashes down around him, he needs to have some say in how to minimize the fallout. What do you think, Fogarty?"

"I agree. He knows the players on the base and we know the players in the city, so we need to share what we've got."

It was a couple minutes after two when the cops strolled into Captain McCain's office.

"Good afternoon, Corporal. How are you this lovely afternoon?" Mouse asked, using his most sarcastic tone of voice.

The sullen NCO ignored Mouse's taunting tone and pointed to the captain's office without even looking up. "You're late. He's in there waiting for you."

Carl knocked and entered the spartan office, shutting the door and noting that the corporal's desk was just outside the closed door.

"I've been anxious to hear what you have to say," Brian quickly interjected.

Carl cautiously looked around the office, pointed to Brian's phone, and quietly suggested, "We had a long drive out here, and it's really a nice day out. Why don't you show us around the base, Captain?"

The others all had quizzical looks on their faces, but Brian sensed that Carl wanted to get out of the office, so he replied, "Sure, that sounds like a good idea. I could use the exercise after being cooped up in the office all day."

As the troupe walked out of the office, Brian said to his surly assistant, "Corporal, we will be back in half an hour or so. Take messages and hold down the fort." With his pun, he winked at Mouse and led them out to the grounds.

"OK, Carl. What was that all about?"

"Brian, how much do you know about Corporal Rollins?"

"Just that he came with the job. He has been running the office since way before I got here."

"Do you trust him?" Carl asked.

"Not particularly. He always seems to be lurking in the background. Furtive, you know what I mean?"

"Brian, when we called you earlier today to set up this meeting, I'm sure Rollins was listening in, and after you hung up, I heard a separate click on the line when he hung up. Not only that: I noticed that the intercom light on your phone was on before we left the office. I think he was listening to every word we said."

"That doesn't surprise me. There have been times when I was suspicious of some caper on the base, but before I could prove it, the bad guys closed down and moved on to something else, like they knew I was on to them. I'm embarrassed to admit that you picked up on that in ten minutes, and I have been letting him get away with it for a long time."

"Don't be embarrassed. Sometimes it takes an outsider to see things that you may take for granted," Carl said. "By the way, for the time being, it may be to our advantage to let Corporal Rollins stay right where he is. Misinformation, you know what I mean? Just be careful what you say when he is around."

"Captain, Carl may think it's a nice day for a walk, but I'm hot and thirsty," Mouse complained. "Is there some shady, air conditioned place we can park our butts?"

The four of them strode over to the Officers' Club, picked up some soft drinks, and garnered a private room where they could talk without being overheard and without tongues starting to wag about Captain McCain meeting with three cops from St. Louis.

"What have you guys found out?" Brian asked impatiently.

The three cops looked at each other, silently questioning who would be the spokesman.

Carl spoke up. "What we have to say is partly fact and partly conjecture, Brian, but I don't think you are going to like any of it.

"It looks as though you were absolutely right about there being a drug connection on base, and you were also right in presuming that the supply starts in St. Louis. Fogarty, since it was your guys who made the connection, why don't you fill Brian in about Faster."

"Who the hell is Faster?" Brian asked.

Fogarty picked up the conversation. "Faster is the street name of a guy we always thought was a low life drug dealer whose real name is Dewayne Foster. He runs around with a goon named Rufus Stoker, who has the moniker

41

Slower. Faster and Slower, get it?

"Anyway, a couple of my guys were keeping an eye on Foster and a foxy girl driving a Beemer convertible with a Fort Leonard Wood parking permit on the front windshield showed up at his condo. She went upstairs for a few minutes, but the real scene was out on the street in front of his place. It was obvious that Faster wanted to shut down the drug supply to the Fort because Carl, Mouse, and I had put some pressure on him, and he was getting nervous about all the attention he was getting. I don't think he wanted to jeopardize the rest of his operation just for this piece of the pie.

"The girl had other ideas," Fogarty continued. "My guys couldn't believe it, but right there out on the street in front of God and the whole world, she goes ballistic, telling him that if he cuts off the supply to the base, she'll get another source. She was probably high on drugs and thoroughly pissed, so she wasn't even aware what she was saying out on a public street."

Brian became very quiet and pensive. "I'm afraid to ask, because I'm not sure I want to know the answer. The only foxy girl with a BMW at Fort Leonard Wood is Lori Newton, the General's daughter. That's who it was, wasn't it?"

"Yes, Brian, that's who it was," Carl replied. "Obviously, we have no proof to take to the State's Attorney yet, but we'll get it. That being said, we need to figure out how to get that evidence and how to minimize the impact on the innocent bystanders. In military terms, you refer to it as collateral damage; in civilian terminology, I call it unintended consequences."

CHAPTER NINETEEN

Because Lori had met Fogarty, Carl, and Mouse, it seemed like a good idea for Carl to bring in some outside surveillance from the State Police to follow her. They picked up her trail later that day, thinking that if she followed through with her threat to Faster to look elsewhere for her drug supply, she would probably do it soon.

Meanwhile, Brian agonized over what to tell General Newton. Since it was his daughter they were talking about, and since the General was responsible for base discipline, Brian had no choice but to bring him up to date.

Brian slowly walked up the brick path to the General's immaculately maintained two story brick home. Even before he rang the bell, Kaitlyn, Lori's identical-but-not-so-identical twin opened the door.

"I saw you coming up the walk, Brian. You look like you have just lost your best friend. What's the matter? Are you okay?"

"No, I'm not okay, Kate," using his favorite name for her. Brian once again marveled at how the two girls were identical in their appearance, but Kate always made those around her feel so good when she entered a room, whereas Lori made them feel so good only when she exited. Beauty is only skin deep, he mused, while ugly goes all the way to the core.

Kate brought him back to the present. "You're not sick, are you?"

"No, Kate, nothing like that. Is the general here?"

"He's in his study, going over some reports. Come on in. Do you want something to drink?"

"No thanks, Kate. I'll just go and talk with him," and he slowly turned down the hallway towards the study.

Brian knocked tentatively on the door to the study.

"Come in, Katlyn."

"It's not Kaitlyn. It's Captain McCain, sir."

"Oh, Brian, I didn't realize the bell rang. Please, come on in. Can I get you something to drink?"

"No thank you, sir. Kate opened the door just before I rang, and she invited me in."

"This doesn't sound like a social call, Brian. What's up?"

"General, do you remember when we talked last week about a possible drug connection to the base and you agreed to let me ask the State Police to investigate?"

"Of course I remember, Brian. I am getting along in years, but I don't have Alzheimer's yet. Have they found something already?"

"General, Carl Watson, the lieutenant from the State Police who told me about my mother's accident, and Sergeant Fogarty from the St. Louis City Police, had a lead on a drug dealer from the city who they thought might be looking to expand his territory, so they had him under surveillance."

Brian was growing more uncomfortable by the minute trying to decide exactly how to break the bad news. Even though Brian knew that Lori had always been a great concern of the general's, he was still her father.

"Sir, I'm not quite sure how to tell you this, but the police are fairly certain that Lori is this dealer's connection to the base." Having finally said it, Brian carefully watched for his mentor's reaction.

General Newton quietly removed his reading glasses and carefully set them atop the pile of official looking papers on his desk. For what seemed like forever, he didn't say a word, but just stared absently at a picture of him, his late wife, and the three- year- old twins which sat prominently at the edge of his desk.

"You know, Brian, even when the girls were young, I knew that Lori was always going to be a challenge. She was always too smart, too sassy, too independent, too much of everything. Her mother and I did everything we could to figure out how two girls, identical in appearance, identical in upbringing, identical in everything we did for them, could end up so differently, even at that early age.

"If it were just Lori," he continued, "that would be bad enough, but Lori being Lori impacted everyone around her. Kaitlyn was, and is, a wonderful daughter, a wonderful person, but I know that she turned out as well as she did in spite of Lori and in spite of me, not because of anything I did for her."

"Sir, with all due respect," Brian interjected, his voice faltering with emotion, "Kate is a very different person from Lori, fortunately, but she has always known the love you have had for her. Remember the story of the Prodigal Son, sir. I always had a problem with that story because the obedient son seems to have gotten screwed. He did everything he was supposed to, but his rebellious brother got all the attention. In the end, though, the good son recognized that his father always loved him, while the father had to learn how

44

to love his other son time and time again.

Brian continued, "It's just like running a business or a military base, General. We spend ninety per cent of our time on the ten per cent of people who are problems, and way too little time on the hard working and reliable staff. Believe me, Kate is just fine, and it's because of you."

"Brian, I know what you are saying, and philosophically I can accept that, but I just look at all the people who have suffered because of Lori. There's Kate, you, your mother, to say nothing of the soldiers on the base who may have been affected by the drugs."

"Sir, Lori has had no bad effect on me at all. You went way overboard to help me, and without you, I would never have gotten accepted at West Point, would never have become a Ranger, would never have had the career you made possible. You have been a father to me, and nothing Lori or anyone else could do will ever change that. Beyond that, I don't know what you mean about Lori hurting my mother."

"Brian, I never told you the whole story about why your mother left Fort Leonard Wood."

"I do know that Lori unjustly accused my mother of taking some of your pain pills, but Mom got over that."

"That was just part of it, Brian. Yes, Lori accused your mother of taking my OxyContin, which I knew was an out and out lie. If that had been all, I would never have asked your mother to leave. But Lori threatened to tell the civilian police that you had tried to rape her unless I got rid of your mother. Even though it was a lie, your mother refused to jeopardize your career over these allegations, even if she couldn't prove anything. Your mother insisted on moving off base. Now you see what I mean about Lori just being an evil person."

Brian sat there, his emotions torn with confusion, anger, and despair. The two men just looked at each other. Call it collateral damage or unintended consequences, it was still a disaster by any name.

After a few minutes, the two professionals got back on track. On the Hermann Brain Dominance scale, they were both blue/green. Just give me the facts and I will develop an action plan, just like putting together a military maneuver.

Brian gave the general the information that they had at the time, including the conversation Lori and Faster Foster had outside his loft and the suspicion about Corporal Rollins. Until they got more hard evidence, however, they agree to keep everything on a need to know basis for the time being.

CHAPTER TWENTY

Lori was beginning to feel the pressure. Never before in her life had she ever had any doubts about anything. She was always supremely confident that whatever she did would always work out to her benefit. Now, she wasn't so sure. Faster was street smart, and if he was nervous about the cops, maybe she should take his advice. But, damn it, she had spent a lot of time and effort setting things up at the base, and she wasn't about to let that all go to waste. That was why she was sitting in her car at 11 o'clock on a pitch black night in the worst part of St. Louis. Her car stood out like a flashing beacon amongst the filthy, dilapidated heaps parked haphazardly along the street. After about ten minutes, two low-riders pulled up, one in front of her and the other close on her trunk, effectively trapping her in this hellhole. The front car flashed the high beams right into her eyes, so she could not see into the intimidating vehicle.

A couple of sharp raps on her driver's side window brought Lori out of her stupor. If she was nervous before, now she was outright scared shitless, but she told herself that she needed to never let them know how scared she was. Otherwise, she would be royally screwed.

"I'm here to meet Ricardo Castillo."

"I know who you are here to meet, Blondie," the thin Chicano responded. Lori carefully looked him over. He had tattoos covering his neck, arms, and upper chest, and he wore a torn sleeveless T-shirt. On the shirt was printed "I HAVE TATTOOS IN PRIVATE PLACES. WANNA SEE 'EM?" Lori began to be more concerned about what she had gotten into, but it was too late to back down now.

"Are you Ricardo Castillo?"

The Chicano just laughed. "You'll meet Ricardo when Ricardo wants you to meet Ricardo," and he carefully peered into her car.

"Get out," he ordered.

"I will not get out," Lori said. Whereupon the intruder opened her door and pulled her out. He then ran his hand over her body, under her blouse, up her skirt between her legs, everywhere. His actions were not sexual, however, so Lori relaxed somewhat.

"No wire," the Chicano said to someone in the front car, and a large man climbed out of the passenger seat. As he became backlit by the headlights, Lori could now see that he was a handsome Mexican American, totally in control.

"I apologize for the manhandling, Miss Newton, but one can't be too careful in this business, can one?"

"How do you know my name?"

"I just told you, didn't I? One can't be too careful. There is no way I was going to meet with someone who contacts me out of the blue and says she wants to buy some drugs. This could be an ambush set up by Faster Foster—you know Faster Foster, I know—or a bust by the cops. Who knows?"

"Are you Ricardo Castillo?"

"At your service, miss."

Although Lori was no longer scared of the man with all the tattoos, Ricardo Castillo was truly a man to be feared. He seemed remarkably intelligent and totally in control. Faster was always frenetic from using the drugs which supported his life style, but Lori seriously doubted whether Castillo had ever touched the stuff.

"Why are you here, Miss Newton? Faster Foster has always been your supplier. What happened? A falling out among thieves?"

"Faster has lost his edge and his balls," Lori replied. "I can't rely upon him to fulfill his end of the bargain, so I am looking for alternatives."

Castillo looked at Lori for what seemed like forever before he replied, "I am willing to consider working with you, but I need to do some background work before we consummate our arrangement."

Consummate our arrangement, Lori thought. This guy sounds more like an MBA graduate from Wharton Business School than a downtown drug dealer from St. Louis. The thought made her even more wary.

As the two of them discussed details of a possible transaction and made arrangements for a follow up meeting, they were unaware of the two black men in the beat up Plymouth Dart parked in the shadows a block away. Although the men couldn't hear any of the conversation, their night vision glasses and photos confirmed that Lori wasn't wasting any time getting her business back on track.

CHAPTER TWENTY--ONE

Since the day that Carl and Mouse entered Missy McCain's home and found her body lying on the floor, Carl had become more taciturn and reflective. Even Mouse, who knew Carl better than anyone in the world, had noted the change in his best friend.

"Carl, something about this case has gotten under your skin. What's the deal?"

"I don't get it, Mouse. Like I said before, there are just too many loose ends, you know? It's like I'm picking at a ball of yarn and I never reach the end. One string just leads to another, and it seems like we are just about to come up with an answer and then some other glitch appears."

"What do you mean, Carl? It seems pretty simple to me. The old lady has an accident, we contact the son, the son realizes we can help him with the drug problem at the base, we find out about the general's crazy drug and sex crazed daughter and her partnership with a St. Louis drug dealer, we shut them down, end of story. I think you're making this more complicated than it needs to be, Carl."

Carl was in the uncomfortable position of doing something he had never done before—keeping relevant information about a case from Mouse. He had become so captivated with what he had learned from Missy McCain's journal that he had decided not to tell Mouse about the journal, at least for now, so any information he learned from the writings he couldn't share.

"Maybe so. Just humor me, though. What if the captain's mother didn't have an accident? Why did she suddenly leave the base and move to St. Louis? What does Corporal Rollins have to do with all this? How much does the general know about what's going on, or is he even somehow involved?"

"I still think you're overthinking this, Carl, but I see where you're coming from. What do you want to do next?"

Carl didn't respond to Mouse right away. He just drove on for awhile. Suddenly, it was as though he had a revelation.

"Mouse, do you remember what the ME said about Missy McCain's death?"

"Sure, he said it was an accident."

"Yes, he said it was an accident," Carl responded, "but do you remember not what he said, but what he wrote in his report?"

"Yeah. He said she had wood splinters in the head wound, splinters which were identical to the coffee table. And the injury caused a subdural hematoma which eventually killed her. But he also wrote that there was a contusion near where she hit her head on the coffee table, which he thought happened when she fell,"

Carl reminded Mouse. "How likely is it that she would hit her head on the coffee table hard enough to knock her out and then bounce and hit her head again hard enough to cause a contusion, or *vice versa*? What if she was hit on the head with some object to knock her out, and then her head slammed into the coffee table to make it look like an accident?"

Mouse thought about that scenario for a while. "It could have happened that way, I guess. I have to admit that as soon as I walked into that house, I was convinced it was an accident, so I really wasn't thinking of other possibilities."

While Carl turned the car around and headed toward Missy McCain's house, Mouse called the ME's office.

"Doc, this is Mouse Brannon. Listen, Carl and I were thinking about that accident case we looked at. You wrote that there was a contusion of the head. Is it likely that the victim would have a severe injury causing the subdural and a separate contusion, or do you think they are two separate injuries?"

The ME hesitated for a moment before he responded. "Mouse, that is an interesting question. I had assumed the two were related to one insult, since they were so close to each other, but I guess they could have been two separate injuries."

"Doc, could you go back and see if there is any contamination of the contusion? I know you found some wood fragments consistent with hitting her head on the coffee table, but could you look for anything else, like metal or paint fragment? You know, that kind of stuff."

"Sure, Mouse, I can review the microscopic slides right away."

After Carl and Mouse arrived at the McCain home, they surveyed the scene with a different eye. Since Brian hadn't had a chance to come in and clean up his mother's home, everything was just as they had left it. Carl felt as though it had been weeks since this case began unfolding in this small living area, but it had been only a matter of days.

Mouse focused on anything that might be used as a weapon, and the Easton baseball bat immediately caught his attention. He carefully inspected the barrel and couldn't see anything obvious, but he put it into a bag to protect any trace evidence.

49

"Good thought, Mouse," Carl interjected. "Have the lab check for blood or tissue on the barrel, but also have them check for prints. Unfortunately, being a dumb shit, I remember picking up the bat and giving it a couple of swings before I put on my gloves, so my prints will probably be on the handle."

Carl and Mouse gathered additional evidence, all of which they now placed in protective bags. "We should have done this the first time, Mouse. The first thing they taught me as a rookie at the Academy was not to investigate anything, an accident, a missing dog, a homicide, anything, without an open mind. Hopefully, this is all a red herring, but we'll see."

While Mouse finished up at the house, Carl stepped out on the porch and called Brian McCain at Fort Leonard Wood. This time, Brian personally answered his phone.

"Captain McCain here."

"Brian, this is Carl Watson. Is Corporal Rollins hanging around there?"

"No, he's out of the office."

"Good. We are at your mother's house, taking a second look at what might have happened."

Brian interrupted him, "Do you think her death was not an accident?"

"We don't know what to think. It certainly looks like she fell off the chair and hit her head, but there a couple of things that don't add up.

"Tell me, Brian, why did your mother suddenly leave the base and move?"

Brian hesitated just an instant. "I met with General Newton this afternoon," Brian began. "I told him everything we know. He didn't seem at all surprised, just disappointed, but he also told me the real reason my mother left the base. She didn't want to talk about it with me, but I eventually got out of her that General Newton had an old back injury, which I knew, and that he kept a small supply of OxyContin around for when the pain became unbearable. He originally started using the Oxy when his wife was dying from cancer and the doctor had prescribed it for her. He never used it much, maybe once or twice a month at most, and his doctor got him his own prescription, so it was all on the up and up. Anyway, the general's nearly full prescription bottle was missing. He confronted Lori, since she was the most likely suspect. Lori adamantly denied taking the bottle and said that she had seen my mother messing around in her father's medicine cabinet. Of course, she cleaned his house religiously, so she had every reason to be in his bathroom. Anyway, they found an empty bottle for OxyContin in my mother's room.

"I was told that the general had no choice but to ask my mother to leave,
50

but he told me today that the real reason she left is that Lori threatened to charge me with attempted rape if my mother wasn't let go. Lori has always been inappropriate around me, not just in private, but also in public. In fact, I have made it a point to avoid being one on one with her. Anyway, both the general and my mother knew she would lie about us, so my mother insisted that she would leave. She did this, Carl, just to protect me."

"Why do you think Lori was so intent on getting rid of your mother, Brian?"

"I think my mother knew what Lori was up to. My mother was a very observant person, Carl. Frequently, people don't even notice the maid quietly doing her work, but my mother would certainly notice what Lori was doing. I'm afraid that my mother was naïve, however. She probably had no idea how dangerous Lori would be when threatened with exposure about her drug dealing. I wouldn't be surprised if my mother actually went to Lori and confronted her. If that were the case, Lori would certainly want her out of the house."

"Thanks, Brian. We'll keep you posted on this end."

CHAPTER TWENTY –TWO

Because of the July 4th holiday, it was two days later before Mouse checked in with the ME.

"Any news, Doc?"

"Yeah, Mouse, I do have some interesting news. When I did some microscopic work on the contusion, I found traces of gray metallic paint. I should have noticed this before, but I have to admit that I was influenced by the fact that we all assumed this was a simple accident. I'm embarrassed that I missed it. If you find anything which matches that, the lab should be able to confirm it. This changes everything, Mouse. I now think that the victim was hit with something with metal paint, not enough to kill her, but enough to stun her, and she then was either hit with the edge of the coffee table or, more likely, her head was hit onto the table if the table was too big to lift. In either case, this looks more and more like homicide."

"Thanks, Doc. We'll let you know if we need anything further."

Mouse turned to Carl.

"I hate it when you are right, because I have to bow and scrape for weeks thereafter," whereupon he filled Carl in on the ME's latest update.

"Mouse, give the lab a visit and see what they came up with on the baseball bat and the other stuff we sent them."

When Mouse came back to the office a couple of hours later, he had a huge grin on his rodent-like face.

"What's with the smile, Mouse, and please don't tell me you went home for a morner," Carl teased.

Mouse had a puzzled look on his face. "What's a morner, Carl?"

"A morner is a nooner only sooner," Carl quipped.

"Hey, that's a good one, Carl. A nooner, only sooner. I get it. Actually, with the news I'm going to give you, I figured you wouldn't mind if I ran by the house for a quickie. You know, to put me in a good mood."

"I'm sorry I even opened the subject. What did you get from the lab, Mouse?"

"Okay. First, there were minute traces of fresh human tissue on the barrel of the bat. Someone tried to wash it off, but they didn't do a very good job of it. They are going to see if it matches Missy McCain, but there is no doubt that it will. Not only that, there were three sets of prints on the handle of the bat—Missy McCain's, yours, and an unknown third person. Your prints were on file, so they could identify yours. I have to say, the guys in the lab had a pretty good chuckle about your prints being on the weapon. I suspect you may get some grief about that."

"Yeah, yeah. What else did you find out?"

"The other thing, Carl, is that there were also prints on the broken light bulb. Just one set of prints, but they were Missy McCain's. It looks like the third person, whoever that was, hit her with the bat and knocked her out, then hit her head on the edge of the coffee table, then purposely broke the light bulb and tipped over the chair to make it look like an accident."

"There was no evidence of a break- in, Mouse, so we have to assume that whoever was at Missy McCain's house was someone she knew and someone she let in. If we think of the players and those people who might have a motive, the list gets pretty short. I think it's time we have a little conversation with Lori Newton, don't you?"

CHAPTER TWENTY—THREE

It was early afternoon by the time Carl and Mouse drove up to the general's home. They had already decided that they were going to intimidate Lori as much as possible, so they planned on bundling her into the back seat of the borrowed black and white, complete with wire mesh separating the two seat benches, locked doors, the whole shebang.

They were relieved to see Lori's flashy Beemer in the driveway, top down, glistening in the bright Midwestern sun, a real trophy car.

After they rang the front bell, Kaitlyn answered the door, at least they were pretty sure it was Kaitlyn, since she was dressed in a demure conservative dress which didn't show any cleavage. They doubted whether Lori Newton had ever dressed like that.

"Kaitlyn, I am Lieutenant Watson and this is Sergeant Brannon. We are from the State Police, and we would like to speak with your sister and your father, please."

"I remember you from Missy's visitation. My dad is at the office, but Lori is here."

"Would you get her for us, please?" Carl asked. He then turned to Mouse and said, "Why don't you call the General and tell him that we will be taking Lori to the office for some questions. Brian already told him what we have found, so I don't think he will be surprised. Try to give him just the bare bones version, though, since we don't know exactly how this will go down. You had better contact Captain McCain also." Mouse nodded and stepped out to the spacious front porch to make the calls.

Lori and Kaitlyn came down the stairs from the second floor, and as Carl gazed upon the identical twins, he couldn't be more aware of how different these spitting images of each other really were. Lori led the procession down the stairs, of course, because Carl was sure she always had to be the center of attention. Her attitude was one of defiance and privilege, despite the fact that Kaitlyn had undoubtedly told her that there were two policemen who wanted to speak with her. Kaitlyn, on the other hand, had nothing to fear, yet her expression was one of confusion and apprehension.

"Miss Newton, Lori Newton that is, I am Lieutenant Watson from the Missouri State Police. My associate and I would like to ask you a few questions."

"Of course , Lieutenant. I would be happy to answer any questions you might have, but what is this in reference to?" Lori replied in her most innocent and condescending tone of voice. "Why don't we go into the living room and sit. Kaitlyn, would you please get us some water or Cokes," Lori demanded, as though she was the lady of the house and Kaitlyn was the hired help.

"That won't be necessary," Carl said. Mouse had returned after contacting Lori's father and Captain McCain, and Carl put on his most business-like voice. "Sergeant, would you please Mirandize Miss Newton."

"Lori Newton, you have the right to remain silent; you have the right to have legal counsel available; if you cannot afford an attorney, one will be provided for you; you may stop answering questions at any time until your attorney is present; anything you say can and will be used against you in a court of law," Mouse recited. "Are you willing to answer questions without an attorney present, Miss Newton?"

"I watch TV, officer; I know the drill, but, really, why all the dramatics?"

Not to be distracted, Mouse had her sign a waiver, stating that she understood and that she didn't want an attorney. Lori then turned toward the living room, her demeanor one of confidence and almost amusement.

Carl intercepted her at the doorway into the well appointed room. "If you would, please come with us, Miss Newton. We will be taking you to headquarters to take your statement."

"My statement about what? Surely you have better things to do than to take me to your headquarters to convince me to contribute to the Policeman's Benevolent Society."

Carl and Mouse got Lori settled into the back of the patrol car, but not comfortably so because the car reeked of disinfectant used to clean out the vomit from the last drunk who sat in the caged section. Lori wasn't sure which was worse, the smell of the disinfectant or the lingering odor of too many sweaty, unwashed bodies. And the damn springs on the bench seat were poking her ass. I don't mind getting my ass poked once in a while, she thought, but not by busted springs in a rundown cop car.

Kaitlyn had followed after the trio as they headed toward the car. She had no idea what was going on behind the scenes, so she was nearly frantic. Although she was acutely aware of her sister's lifestyle, it still was a shock to see her twin sitting in the back of a police car.

"Where are you taking her? What do you want with her? You need to

55

tell my father what is happening," she exclaimed.

"Kaitlyn, Sergeant Brannon has spoken with your father and with Captain McCain. We are taking her to our office to answer a few questions regarding an ongoing investigation. Your father can fill you in on the details. He should be on his way as we speak," Carl explained.

Carl and Mouse then stepped away so they could have a private conversation. They wanted Lori to sit isolated in the car for a few minutes to see whether she would soften up some, but Mouse watched her through the back side window. "Look at her, Carl, sitting there like she is Queen for a Day. More like Bitch for a Day. You talk about an ice princess."

"More like Fire and Ice, I suspect," Carl observed. "There is a lady who has to be in complete control. The only way we will get anything out of her is if she loses control, and I'm not sure that is going to happen."

CHAPTER TWENTY-- FOUR

Lori kept up a constant banter on the drive into the police headquarters. She acted as though she were on a date with a couple of cute guys. This just made Mouse madder and Carl more concerned. Mouse felt as though she was using them rather than the other way around. When Lori made a suggestion that the three of them pick up some wine and cheese and have their conversation at Forest Park, Mouse almost lost it.

"This is not a *ménage a trois,* Miss. This is a police investigation, and you are up shit creek without a paddle, so, if I were you, I would be more cooperative," he said.

"Why, Sergeant, I have been more than cooperative," Lori responded, again with her most innocent, yet seductive, manner. "In fact, I would be happy to cooperate with you and Lieutenant Watson in any way you can imagine."

Carl turned and gave Mouse the look which silently said, "Ignore her. She's just getting under your skin." In reality, Carl, too, was becoming more concerned, but for a different reason. He really doubted whether Lori Newton had any remorse for anything she had done. More importantly, he was concerned that they may not be able to convince the State's Attorney or a jury of any of the allegations.

Once they arrived at headquarters, the three of them went up the dingy stairwell to the second floor. As usual, the large room where a dozen overworked detectives shared cubicle space was rife with ringing phones, loud voices, and organized chaos. Each of the numerous identical institutional looking grey metal desks was covered with stacks of papers, photos, and binders holding documents pertaining to the never ending influx of crimes facing the squad.

The Bullpen, as it was called by its over-androgenic inhabitants, became eerily quiet as Carl and Mouse led the striking blonde into Interrogation Room #3. Carl heard a hushed, "Holy shit. I would love to interrogate that fox for hours."

Lori turned to where the voice originated and gave the detective a thousand watt smile and a wink that probably made the guy come right there into his boxers. She then went into the interrogation room, carefully rearranged her thigh- high skirt, turned to Carl, and said, "Now, Lieutenant, how may I help you?"

"Miss Newton," Carl began, "I want to tell you that this interview is being videotaped and recorded. Also, I want to confirm that Sergeant Brannon has read you your rights and that you have declined the presence of an attorney, is that correct?"

"That is correct. I have no reason to have an attorney, Lieutenant."

Carl and Mouse had decided to start with the most serious charge, the killing of Missy McCain.

"Miss Newton, were you acquainted with Missy McCain, the mother of Captain Brian McCain, and your housekeeper at Fort Leonard Wood?"

"Of course I knew Missy. She was our housekeeper and our nanny for as long as I can remember."

"Missy McCain left your father's employ rather suddenly some time ago, Miss Newton."

"Please call me Lori, Lieutenant. Miss Newton makes me sound so old and dowdy."

"Miss Newton," Carl sternly replied, refusing to let her control the interview, "if we can continue, do you know why Ms. McClain left so suddenly?"

"I do know that some of my father's pain medications were taken from his bathroom cabinet and that the empty container was found in Missy's room. My father felt as though he had no choice but to dismiss her. She had been a lifelong employee, so my father did not want to file any charges, but he did not feel he could trust her any longer. Surely you understand that."

"What if I were to tell you that your father has said that he believes you took those pills and planted the empty bottle in Ms. McClain's room to incriminate her? What if I were to tell you that your father says you insisted he fire her or else you would destroy her son's career by telling the authorities that Brian had tried to rape you? That was why Missy McCain was let go."

"Lieutenant, my father must have misunderstood me. I did tell him that Brian came on to me inappropriately and that I felt uncomfortable being around him, but I never said that he had tried to rape me. After all, the only difference between rape and consensual sex is salesmanship, and Brian would be an excellent salesman, I am sure, if he put his mind to it."

Mouse winced in the background, but a firm glance from Carl made Mouse settle back into his chair.

"Moving along, Miss Newton, we have evidence indicating that Missy

McCain did not have an accident." However, Carl didn't explain that the evidence was only suggestive at this point, not definitive.

"Oh, that's terrible. Why would someone want to kill Missy?"

"I didn't say that she was killed, Miss Newton. Why do you think that she was?"

"Lieutenant, don't play silly word games with me. There are only four ways a person could die—homicide, suicide, an accident, or from some disease. Missy McCain had no disease that I know of, and if that caused her death, the police would not be involved. You said it wasn't an accident and there is no way she would commit suicide, especially by hitting her head on a piece of furniture. Too unpredictable, you know. Therefore, you must think she was killed."

Thus far, Carl had been the good cop, the Jack Webb from *Dragnet* "just the facts, ma'am" type cop. Mouse now jumped in. He was going to be the bad cop.

"Listen, lady, we found traces of Ms. McClain's tissue on the business end of the baseball bat sitting against the wall. Not only that, we found your fingerprints on the handle of the bat and also on the light bulb which was broken on the floor," not explaining that they had identified the fingerprints on the bulb as belonging to the victim.

"We know what happened that day," he continued. "You went over to talk with Missy McCain because you wanted to find out how much she knew about your drug trafficking at the base. Unfortunately, she told you what she knew. Even more unfortunately for her, she underestimated what a cold bitch she was dealing with. You saw Captain Newton's Little League bat sitting against the wall. You hit her with the bat and knocked her unconscious. You then slammed her head against the coffee table, as hard as you could because you had to make sure that she wasn't just stunned. You wanted her dead. Once you knew that she was a goner, you staged the chair and the light bulb to make it look like an accident."

"Why, Sergeant, what a vivid imagination you have! First, I did not go to see Missy McCain. I have never been to her house. Secondly, I have no idea what you are referring to when you talk about drugs at the base. Thirdly, my sister, Kaitlyn, my identical sister I would remind you, told me that she was going to help Missy unpack her belongings at her new house. Kaitlyn was always close to Missy. In fact, Kaitlyn was always a do-gooder. The fingerprints on the baseball bat probably got there when she helped Missy

59

unpack. She is my identical sister, after all, so her prints are the same as mine," not realizing that identical twins have different fingerprints. "Or maybe I touched the bat one night when I slept over," she said, a smug grin on her face. "And the prints on the light bulb are probably hers also. She probably put in a new bulb when Missy first moved in."

"The prints on the light bulb were on the inside of a broken piece, Miss Newton, not on the outside," Mouse responded.

"Inside, outside, I don't know how Kaitlyn's prints got there. Maybe you should ask her. Maybe she killed Missy," Lori replied with a smug smile.

"Miss, Newton…"

"I prefer Lori, Lieutenant."

Uninterruptedly, Carl continued, "As I was saying, Miss Newton, do you know a man named Dewayne Foster, known on the street as Faster Foster?"

"Yes, I know Dewayne. He and I are working together to provide toys and playground equipment for inner city kids."

Mouse jumped up from his chair and walked aimlessly around the small interrogation room. "I haven't heard this much bullshit since the last Presidential election."

Lori looked at him and again smiled. "Yes, those politicians are full of shit. Not only that, they never do what's best for the people, only what's best for them. Mr. Foster and I decided that we could do a lot of good if we could do something to help the kids on the street get off the street and onto a more constructive path."

"Miss Newton, we have evidence that you and Faster Foster had a disagreement and you accused him of being a ball-less asshole—your words, not mine—who reneged on a drug deal. You were going to look for another supplier and dump him."

"I don't know where you got this so-called evidence, Lieutenant. Yes, I do have a rather fiery temper. Mr. Foster was trying to back out of our arrangement to provide for the kids. That ticked me off, especially since we were so close to achieving our goal, so I told him I would find someone else to work with. Believe me, it had nothing to do with drugs, only swings, slides, and teeter-totters," she laughed.

"Now, if you have no other fanciful topics of discussion, perhaps you could arrange for someone to take me home. Unless you intend to arrest me, of course," whereupon Lori stood up, looked Carl squarely in the eyes, and challenged him to do otherwise.

Carl arranged for a patrol car to take Lori back to Fort Leonard Wood while he and Mouse decided upon their next move.

"Mouse," Carl said, "I think we need to go see Faster Foster again. When we put pressure on him before, he began to panic, so let's see how far we can push him again."

After arriving at Faster's building, they were again ushered upstairs by Slower Stover, but Faster was more subdued and ill-appearing than he had been only four days earlier.

Mouse got right into Faster's face, as he and Carl had discussed on the ride over from their office. "Okay, asshole, we know all about you and that broad from the army base. You might as well come clean about the drug setup you have going with her."

Faster, however, managed to maintain his cool. "Sergeant, I don't appreciate your barging into my home and making these wild accusations. If you are referring to my relationship with Lori Newton from Fort Leonard Wood, she and I are discussing a philanthropic venture to provide playground equipment and toys for inner city kids, nothing else."

Carl, as planned, interceded before Mouse became more aggressive. "Faster, you and I both know that is a bunch of crap. Just be aware that we will be watching you.

"Come on, Mouse, let's get out of here."

As they were leaving, Carl turned to Faster and politely asked if he could use the restroom before they hit the road.

"Just wait until your prostate starts acting up like mine, Faster. You'll find you take of every opportunity you can to hit the head."

"Sure, Lieutenant, you know where the bathroom is. Help yourself."

Carl entered the well-appointed bathroom and found it just as it had been—an uncapped tube of toothpaste and a bottle of Scope mouthwash on the marble countertop; used condoms and Kleenex saturated with clotted blood in the fancy waste can. Carl did what he came to do, washed up, and returned to the entryway, where Mouse was waiting.

"Let's go, Mouse. See you around, Faster—real soon, I suspect," Carl said, with a sly smile.

CHAPTER TWENTY—FIVE

The next day, Carl and Mouse spent the better part of the morning chasing down loose ends. They had some of the local cops ask the neighbors around Missy McCain's house whether they had seen any unusual traffic or cars around her place over the past several weeks, specifically a flashy BMW. The neighborhood was comprised primarily of retired folks who lived in small, but well- maintained, bungalows. By and large, though, they were pretty observant and looked after each other, almost like an unofficial Neighborhood Watch program. Unfortunately, none of them were in the income tax bracket where they would be shopping for a Beemer, but none recognized the photo that the officers showed them.

Mouse called Kaitlyn Newton to verify Lori's contention that Kaitlyn had helped Missy move into her new digs. Kaitlyn confirmed that she had, but she didn't remember handling the baseball bat, and she certainly did not remember replacing any light bulbs, especially any broken ones.

One interesting development, however, was that the lab called Mouse and told him that the fingerprint pattern on the baseball bat showed that the swinger's left hand was above the right, suggesting either a backhanded grip, which was unlikely, or a left hander. Kaitlyn confirmed that she was right handed, but she told Mouse that Lori had a spiral fracture of her right forearm when she fell from a 25- foot tree at age 6, so she had become ambidextrous thereafter. Unlike Kaitlyn, who was more inclined to be at the library than on the baseball diamond, Lori had turned into a pretty good softball player and had retained her left- handed batting stance so she could get a quicker step to first base.

Carl and Mouse both were skeptical of whether they had enough hard evidence on Lori for the State's Attorney to take to the Grand Jury, but they decided to take what they had to the S.A.

That afternoon, Carl, Mouse, Fogarty, and Brian McCain all gathered in the spacious office of Robert (don't ever call me Bob) Jameson, State's Attorney for the County of St. Louis. Jameson had been S.A. for nearly two decades. He was a political animal who had the uncanny ability to morph from a liberal Democrat who was seen with the pols from the African American community when the political winds made it advantageous to do so, to a conservative Republican when the temperament of the voters shifted rightward. He retained his largely political position not because of any greatlegal ability but because he knew the right people and because, according to rumors, he knew where everyone's skeletons were buried. Not only did he know where the skeletons were buried, he reportedly was more than willing to use that knowledge to keep the movers and shakers in line. In fact, he made no bones of the fact that J. Edgar Hoover was his idol.

The State's Attorney office was charged with prosecuting capital crimes, among others, but the real work was done not by Robert Jameson, Esq., but by the minions who actually knew the law and had been inside a courtroom in the past 20 years. Jameson, however, decided which cases to prosecute, which to plead out, and which to dismiss, and he never prosecuted a case unless he was 100 per cent sure of winning. That way, he could brag on his high conviction rate when he had to go out campaigning every four years.

Jameson's Executive Assistant (don't ever call me a Secretary) led the foursome into a huge conference room, twice as large as the bullpen back at headquarters, which housed 12 detectives at a time on any given day, As the lady who showed them into the inner sanctum, she made a great show of pointing out the gallery of pictures adorning the far wall, each showing her boss with a different political figure. Mouse couldn't help but notice the attractive thirty- something- year- old with the shapely legs and great rack, accentuated by a tight fitting blouse that let one's imagination run amok. He smirked and wondered if Bobby boy, the big boss, had ever laid the hired help on the thirty-foot polished mahogany table which spanned the room. If not on the table, at least somewhere, he was sure.

The group waited for a good twenty minutes before the Grand Poopah himself made his appearance. He was coatless and glanced at his watch before saying, without any greeting whatsoever, "I have a busy schedule this morning. What is this about?" By his tone, Jameson was already mentally moving on to his next appointment, probably some political duty. His salt and pepper hair was thinning, but a $200 haircut had skillfully covered up the balding spots. His dress shirt was so white it was almost blinding, and it was so heavily starched that Mouse figured Jameson could probably take it off and it would stand up by itself in the corner until he put it back on.

Carl introduced the others and gave a recap of both the presumed murder and the drug situation at Fort Leonard Wood. Jameson asked a few questions,

63

all the time not so surreptitiously looking at his watch.

"Lieutenant, I don't care about a drug problem at Leonard Wood. That's their problem and not under the jurisdiction of my office."

"With all due respect, sir," Carl interjected, "you could argue that you have jurisdiction if the source of the drugs is here in St. Louis."

"Yes, I could argue that if I wanted to do so, but at least at this time, I don't want to take on a bullshit drug case. You don't have any concrete evidence against anyone on the drug case, and you don't even know if that McClure lady…."

"McCain, sir, her name is McCain," Mouse interrupted.

Jameson gave Mouse an icy glare and said, "McCain, McClure, whatever. In either case, you don't even know that it wasn't an accident. Get some real evidence and then you can speak with Aaron Levine, my Chief Deputy. Otherwise, you are just wasting my time." With that, he rose and left the room with nary a nod.

The four of them just looked at each other. Fogarty was the first to respond. "I hope this room isn't wired," he whispered in a voice so quiet that the others could barely hear but which no microphone could possibly pick up, "but I wouldn't put it past him. Now you see why every cop in St. Louis hates this guy. All he is interested in is his next reelection and taking the easy way out. None of us feel like he has our back at all."

Fogarty's warning about the room possibly being wired kept the others quiet until they got outside the building.

Brian was livid. "I don't believe that guy. He is willing to let my mother's killer just walk away. Hell, he isn't even interested enough to remember her name for five fucking minutes."

Carl tried to calm Brian down. "I know how you feel, Brian. I feel the same, but you can fight City Hall only so much. We need to figure out some way to get someone to turn on Lori. Maybe if we put some pressure on Corporal Rollins, he may fold."

"Rollins is not a major player in the big scheme of things, Carl," Brian replied. "It's worthwhile talking with him, but it's my mom's murder that I want to nail Lori on."

"We'll figure something out, Brian. Believe me, I am just as anxious to avenge your mother's murder as you are. Just let me think about it for a while."

All four of them were so spent that they figured they would just get a fresh start in the morning, and they agreed to get together by phone following day. However, as events unfolded they would be talking way before then.

CHAPTER TWENTY—SIX

Carl returned to his small apartment. It was a typical bachelor place on the second floor of a complex which surrounded on three sides an oval swimming pool. The pool was virtually uninhabited during the week, but on weekends was teeming with guys trying to hustle girls and girls wearing the skimpiest of bathing suits, making it easier for the guys. Carl was not into the singles scene and his hours made him very much an outsider among his neighbors. He got along fine with them, but he just didn't have anything in common with them. Some of the guys tried to fix him up with girls they knew ("leftovers," Carl suspected), and he had occasionally been invited to get-togethers, but after he declined time after time, the invitations stopped. Carl thought it was too much trouble to look for somewhere else to live and the people were nice enough, so he just stayed.

When he entered his stuffy apartment, Carl whipped off his necktie, turned up the air conditioner, and threw a Lean Cuisine into the microwave. He figured that with all the crap he ate during the day, he should at least pretend to eat something healthy once in a while, and the dinners were easy and pretty tasty, all things considered.

He popped open a Bud Light while he waited for the dinner to heat up, sat in the recliner and just stared out the sliding glass door which opened to a small balcony overlooking the pool.

Carl was frustrated and angry, a little of both, but he grew more angry and less frustrated as he thought about Missy McCain, Lori Newton, and all the players. Just about then, he heard the microwave ding, so he retrieved his dinner, popped another brew, and sat down to watch the Cardinals game, hoping to forget about work for a few hours.

The alarm had been set for 6:00 the next morning, but Carl kept drifting in and out of a restless attempt at sleep. At 2:00 a.m., however, he was rudely awakened by the beep of his pager and almost simultaneously by the shrill ringing of his landline phone. He answered the phone first.

"Carl, it's Mouse. I paged you also, so you can forget that. We have a problem."

"Jesus Christ, Mouse, it's two a.m., I haven't slept a wink, and we're not on call. What's the big emergency?"

"The security guys at Forest Park just found a car out there and there's a dead body in it, Carl. It's Lori Newton."

Carl instantly was fully awake. "Oh, fuck, Mouse, what the hell is going on? Where exactly are you?"

"I'm in the north parking lot next to the Muny Opera at Forest Park. You won't miss the black and whites and the lights. Get over here as soon as you can."

"I'll be there in twenty minutes. Make sure some rookie doesn't screw up the scene for us."

"Already on it," Mouse responded.

CHAPTER TWENTY—SEVEN

Carl had no trouble finding the scene. He was very familiar with the Municipal Opera outdoor theater at Forest Park, of course, since he had spent many a warm summer evening taking in the productions at the hillside location. The Muny, as it was known, had been a St. Louis summer staple for ages.

There were three black and white patrol cars, the bars of light on their roofs like a beacon in the muggy black night. Mouse had completed a preliminary survey of the situation just as Carl arrived. The Medical Examiner was not there yet, Mouse told Carl, but he was on his way.

As he always did at a crime scene, with the exception of Missy McCain's, Carl stepped back and took in the general impression of the scene. Sometimes, that would give Carl a real sense of what might have happened. Only then did he approach Lori's car. It was parked haphazardly in the far corner of the otherwise empty lot, with the exception of all the cop cars. The driver's side door was open, and she was sitting upright in the driver's seat, slumping against the head rest. The most striking thing, however, was that Lori didn't look nearly as appealing now, as a corpse, as she had the last time Carl saw her. There was no blood to speak of, at least that he could see, but her face was bloated and grotesque, with her swollen tongue protruding from her mouth. She always had looked so cool, so composed, so in control whenever Carl had seen her, but her final "death mask" was one of a person who knew, just for an instant before she died, that she was a goner. It was an expression of abject fear. Although Carl had never particularly liked Lori and he would have done whatever it took to put her away for what she had done, it still bothered him to see her like this.

Carl turned to Mouse and Fogarty. "What do we know so far?"

Mouse looked at his notes. "The Rent-A-Cops that the Muny uses made rounds after the performance of *Mama Mia*, which ended right at 10:30. They always hang around after the performance to make sure there is no mischief and to help the cast or anyone in the audience who may have car trouble, you know? Anyway, by 11:15 the lot was clear, the cast and technicians were all gone, and the place was locked up as tight as a drum. At quarter to one, they noticed Lori's Beemer sitting over here, with the driver's door open. They came over to check it out and found her just like you see her. Although they are not regular cops, both of them used to be on the job, so they know the procedure. They backed away, preserved the scene and called it in. The city guys knew that Fogarty was looking into Lori Newton, so they called him."

"I wasn't on call, but our guys always call whoever is running the case if something like this happens," Fogarty explained. "I was out in the County, so I called Mouse and asked him to hustle over here until I could get here, which he did."

"We can check better in the daylight," Mouse continued, "but there are no obvious tire tracks or footprints. The ME can give us the cause of death, but it looks like she was strangled. Based on what the security guys say with the car, it looks like the time of death was sometime between 11:15 and 12:45, but the ME can confirm that."

"Have the CSI guys been here yet, Mouse?" Carl asked.

"They're pulling in right now."

"Fogarty, I think we have to assume that this is somehow related either to the drug stuff going on at the base or to the murder of Missy McCain. Although it is technically a City case, I think it would best if we took over, since the State Police can cross over several jurisdictions and since we have been in on the case from the beginning. Of course, Mouse and I would want you to continue to work with us on this. You okay with that?"

"Hell, yes, I'm okay with that. I've got more than enough on my plate, but I would like to follow through with this."

"Okay, we've got that little technicality resolved. Let's see what the CSI guys can tell us."

Carl and the others stayed out of the way while the technicians from the Crime Scene Investigation unit went about bagging Lori's hands to preserve any trace evidence, vacuuming her car, taking prints, all the requisite procedures which are so important in helping to identifying the perp and building a case.

"Lieutenant, come look at this," one of the techs hollered to Carl.

On the backside of the driver's head rest was a streak of rust colored stain, dried but looking all the world like blood.

'The Luminol picked it up," the tech explained. "We got a good sample of it, so you should be able to compare the DNA if you can find a suspect, Lieutenant."

The CSI team meticulously combed through the car, tires, interior, trunk, everything, and they then packed up and left. Meanwhile, the ME had arrived with his van. He had done his own photographs of the body, although the CSI had taken dozens of their own pictures, taken a body temperature to help confirm the time of death, and done a superficial examination.

"I will be able to give you a much better idea after we check the body out at the morgue and do the autopsy," he said, "but I would be surprised if we don't find that she died of strangulation. She has a cut around her neck, like she had been garroted from behind. She also has petechial hemorrhages of the conjunctiva, consistent with strangulation. Her nose seems to have been broken, so I suspect she may have been punched in the face, and the assailant then went around behind her and strangled her. The marks on her neck are most consistent with strangulation from behind, rather than from the front."

"Why do you think he went into the back seat to strangle her?" Mouse asked. "He had already punched her. Why not just take the wire or whatever he used, slip it over her head and get her from the front?"

"Two reasons I can think of, Mouse," the ME answered. "First, I doubt that a punch to the nose would render her unconscious, so by going behind her, she would have a hard time resisting him. Secondly, many killers, particularly with strangulation or other more personal attacks, want to distance themselves psychologically from the victim. You know, 'out of sight, out of mind.' By not having to look at the victim's face, the assailant can be more detached from the act, you know what I mean?"

"Do you think the blood on the back of the head rest belongs to the perp or to the victim, Doc?" Fogarty asked.

"There was very little blood from the broken nose," he responded. "Also, I don't see how blood from the victim's nose would likely end up on the back of the head rest. I suspect the assailant may have bled onto the head rest without him even being aware of it. We will test the blood, of course. I may not be able to tell you who it belongs to, unless you can get me a comparative sample, but I will be able to tell you whether it belonged to the victim."

As the ME loaded the body into his van, Carl turned to Mouse and Fogarty. "Do you remember when we were up in Faster Foster's condo how he kept having those nose bleeds? Makes you wonder, doesn't it?"

CHAPTER TWENTY—EIGHT

Carl and Mouse wrapped up what they could accomplish at that hour of the morning. They made sure Fogarty had a black and white stay at the scene to keep any "looky-sees" away and to keep the scene intact until the CSI guys could do further evaluation by the light of day. Both of them knew that their adrenaline rush would keep them from getting any useful sleep, so they went back to the office to figure out what the hell just happened.

"Jeez, Carl, I know that we all wanted that broad to go down for what she had to have done, but I didn't expect someone to kill her. If she killed McCain's mother, why would someone else want her out of the way, unless she had an accomplice who was getting nervous that she may roll over on him? Or maybe we were wrong and she didn't kill Missy McCain and the real murderer is still out there? If that were the case, though, why kill her, since she would probably have taken the fall for him?"

"Lori Newton killed Missy McCain, Mouse," Carl somberly replied. "I would bet my shield on it. I think she was killed not because of the McCain murder, but because of drugs, either a drug deal gone bad or, more likely, because she was bringing too much attention to the drug trade. Think about it, Mouse. Dewayne Foster, Ricardo Castillo, all those guys who have been running the drug trade in St. Louis for a long time had a great gig going. Yeah, there were occasional turf wars, but they took care of those problems themselves, and the cops were content to let them control their own gangs as long as they kept civilians out of it. There was peace on the street, if you know what I mean. Then Lori Newton came along and opened new territory for the rivals to fight over. Despite that, Faster Foster seemed to have moved into the new drug market at the army base without a lot of resistance from the competition. He was working well below the radar screen until Brian McCain asked us to get involved. All of a sudden, the spotlight was now on Foster. When the heat started getting turned up, Foster wanted to take a low profile and cool it, but Lori brought Castillo into the mix. Now, everybody was getting nervous because this could start a new gang war or, worse, it could get the cops looking into their business more than they wanted. Somebody, then, decided the best solution was to eliminate Lori and go back to how things were before she stirred the pot."

"You think Faster killed Lori, Carl?" Mouse asked.

"Yeah, I think that's exactly what happened. I think we should pull Foster and Castillo in for a chat, but I'm putting my money on Foster."

Carl and Mouse picked up Ricardo Castillo. He was, as usual, calm, cool, and collected. He admitted to meeting with Lori Newton earlier that week, but his story was the same as Lori's, that they were looking to provide toys and playground equipment for inner city kids since Dewayne Foster had backed out of the deal.

"After all, Lieutenant, I feel as though it is my civic duty to give back to those who are less fortunate than I, especially since I have been so fortunate to have a modicum of success in my business ventures," Castillo explained, with a sardonic smile on his face.

They were unable to get any useful information from the handsome Chicano, so they let him go.

They then drove over to Faster Foster's condo. Slower Stoker was guarding the private entrance.

"Good morning, Rufus," Mouse pleasantly greeted the ape. "We are here to see Faster."

"I'll see if he is available," Slower grumbled, and he called upstairs. After he hung up the phone, the two policemen were escorted to the elevator.

When they were greeted upstairs by Faster, Carl explained that they wanted to take him downtown to ask him a few questions. Faster asked, "What is this all about, Lieutenant?"

Carl explained, "Lori Newton was murdered last night and we want to talk to you about it."

Faster was obviously taken back by this unexpected news, but he recovered quickly.

"Am I under arrest, Lieutenant, because I was right here all last night, and I barely knew Lori Newton."

"Yeah, Faster, I know. You were just providing toys for kids. That's the party line, right? We just have some questions to ask, Faster, that's all."

"Tell you what, Lieutenant, I'll call my attorney and ask him to come by and pick me up and we will meet you at your office in, say, an hour and a half. How about that?"

Carl thought for a minute. "Okay, Faster, 90 minutes at my office. Come on, Mouse, we'll make a couple stops in the meantime."

When they were back on the road, Mouse asked, "Carl, why did you let Faster lawyer up, rather than dumping him in the back seat and making him

72

sweat for a while?"

"Faster doesn't rattle very easily, Mouse, and he was going to contact his mouthpiece anyway, so I figured we would throw him a bone and let him think he is controlling this meeting. Maybe he'll give us something if he thinks we're just fishing. Besides, I wanted to drop by the ME's office and see if he has anything for us."

As they walked into the ME's office, they saw him huddled over a microscope. Books, trays of slides, and stacks of papers were strewn everywhere in the small hideaway. There was no place to sit, so Carl lifted several large tomes off the only chair in the room other than the pathologist's ancient swivel that squeaked with every movement.

"Any news on the Newton case, Doc?" Carl asked.

"Not much yet. The pattern of the strangulation seems to confirm what I said last night. We know the blood type from the smear on the back of the headrest. It doesn't match the victim. If you can get me a sample for comparison, we have plenty to do DNA testing. One thing, though. From the scatter appearance of the blood smear, it appears as though it didn't spontaneously drip and hit the cushion. It looks like it may have been on another substance, probably a tissue, and was then transferred secondarily to the head rest."

"You mean like he blew his nose, and then the Kleenex rubbed against the head rest?"

"Yeah, Mouse, something like that would explain it."

"We have a suspect who is a long time coke user, Doc," Carl explained. Every time we see him, he is constantly wiping his nose and there is a bunch of blood on the tissue. I'm thinking that he may be good for this."

"Carl, if you get me a sample from one of those tissues, I will be able to tell you for sure whether it came from him or not."

"We'll get that for you, Doc. You can count on it." With that, they went back to the office to meet with Faster Foster.

Precisely ninety minutes after they had left Foster's condo, Faster sauntered into the State Police headquarters accompanied by a jet black man with slicked back wavy hair, kept in place, Mouse was sure, by a half jar of expensive pomade.

Faster made an extravagant introduction. "Lieutenant Watson, Sergeant Brannon, this is Pierre Maisson, my attorney." The elegant counselor offered his hand to the policemen, and they responded in kind.

Pierre Maisson was well known to every cop in St. Louis. His original

73

name was Grover Jones, from Lafayette parish in Louisiana. He somehow graduated from a second rate law school in his home state and moved to St. Louis 10-12 years earlier. When he relocated, he had his name legally changed to Pierre Maisson and advertised to every pimp and whore he could find. He bragged that his parents knew he was destined to have a career in law so they named him after Perry Mason, and he became the "French Cajun attorney of choice."

To say that Pierre Maisson was flamboyant would be an understatement. He wore patent leather black and grey shoes with two inch elevated translucent heels. The heels were filled with water, and each held a goldfish swimming comfortably, shimmering with each step, a style made famous by Frenchy Fuqua, the iconic Pittsburgh Steelers running back of the 1970's. Maisson drove a titty-pink Cadillac which was the original property of a top selling Avon salesperson. He got the car as payment for his rather exorbitant fee when she was accused of not only selling cosmetics to the ladies of the house but also selling herself to the men of the house. Apparently, the men were much more tolerant of their wives' shopping when they got to do their own "shopping," as it were.

Faster and his attorney were led into a dank poorly lit interrogation room. They settled into unpadded wooden chairs which, unbeknownst to them, had a half inch of the front legs shaved off, so the chairs tilted forward, just to make the occupant more uncomfortable. Carl and Mouse sat on the opposite side of the table.

Carl started the tape recorder sitting on the table and identified the date, time, place, and who was present. The video camera had been recording since the quartet first entered the room. He then recited the Miranda mantra, although Maisson objected. Carl went one step beyond the usual Miranda warning. He added, "Anything you say or do can and will be used against you." The two words "or do" were specifically inserted so Faster or his attorney could not object later if they picked up any trace evidence during the interrogation. Carl completed the Miranda procedure and began.

"Mr. Foster, could you tell us where you were between 11:00 p.m. and 1:00 a.m. last night?"

"My client has a right to know why you are asking, Lieutenant."

"Of course, Counselor. Last night, an acquaintance of Mr. Foster, Lori Newton, was found dead in the parking lot of the Municipal Opera in Forest Park. It appears as though she was murdered. Mr. Foster was recently seen and heard arguing with Miss Newton outside his building. It is known that the two

74

of them have had a recent falling out because Mr. Foster had reneged on an arrangement in supplying drugs for resale to Miss Newton."

Carl had conveniently left a box of Kleenex on the table, with a waste can sitting within reach of Faster's chair. Faster' had already gone through at least a half dozen of the tissues, each heavily saturated with fresh blood as he continually wiped his bloody nose.

"Lieutenant, my client was at home from 7:00 p.m. last night until 8:30 this morning, when he left to check on some of his business interests. Moreover, he has never dealt in drugs with Miss Lori Newton or anyone else. His only relationship with Miss Newton is as a friend and as a possible co-sponsor of a philanthropic program for disadvantaged children. Miss Newton wanted to take the program in a different direction than my client thought was most cost effective, so, yes, they did have a mild disagreement on the subject. There certainly was no conspiracy, which you are suggesting."

Carl knew that they would not get any further information, so they ended the conversation. Both he and Mouse waited anxiously as Faster and Maisson prepared to leave, hoping that the attorney did not see through the ulterior motive the policemen had. Fortunately, neither of the departing men had the foresight to gather up the soiled tissues and take them with them.

Mouse took a deep breath, smiled, and quickly bundled up the bloody tissues in an evidence bag. "I'll get this right over to the ME," he said, and he quickly went down the back stairs to the parking garage.

CHAPTER TWENTY—NINE

The next several days were spent attending to routine office duties while Carl and Mouse anxiously awaited DNA typing on the samples they had delivered to Dr. Boyle, the ME. In years past, it took weeks, if not months, to get results of DNA testing, but with the new technology the turnover time was a matter of days. Every morning , Mouse called the ME with the same question, "Any news yet, Doc?", and the response from the usually very patient medic became more terse each day, until finally Dr. Boyle admonished Mouse.

"Mouse, you're becoming a pain in the butt. I put your case at the head of the list, and I told you I would call you as soon as we have some results, so quit bugging me every damn day. I can't get any work done because I'm always on the phone with you."

Mouse was uncharacteristically apologetic. "I'm sorry, Doc. I won't call again, but Carl and I just want to make sure we get the guy who killed that girl, even though she may have deserved it."

"I know, Mouse, you are just trying to do your job, but for crying out loud, leave me alone so I can do mine," and he hung up.

While they were primarily investigating the Lori Newton murder, Carl was convinced that Lori had killed Missy McCain. Although Lori was their primary focus, he also wanted to bring closure to the McCain case, so he and Mouse decided to put some pressure on Corporal Rollins, who they felt was intimately involved with the drug trade at the base and who might know something about the McCain murder.

Carl drove down to Fort Leonard Wood and met with Brian McCain and General Newton to bring them up to date on the evidence in both of the ongoing investigations. Initially, Brian had refused to accept the possibility that Lori may have intentionally targeted his mother, but as Carl had rolled out all the circumstantial facts they had, Brian had become more convinced that she was responsible.

"Carl, proving that Lori killed my mother will not bring my mother back; and I certainly don't want to cause you more anguish than you are already feeling, General, but we owe it to my mother to get to the truth."

"Son," General Newton responded, "and I use the term with great affection toward you, Lori was my daughter, and I loved her unconditionally because she was my daughter, but I must admit that although I loved her, I didn't like who she had become. I didn't like who she was, how she acted, or how she treated all those people around her, especially your mother, who cared for her and loved her. Yes, we absolutely need to find the truth, and, Lieutenant, I will help any way I can to do so."

General Newton left, and Brian brusquely used his intercom to summon Corporal Rollins.

"Corporal, would you please come in here?"

"Yes, sir."

Corporal Rollins looked like a soldier who had been on three day shore leave without sleep. His usually immaculate uniform was in disarray. He was even more sullen than Carl had seen previously, which was saying something. Mostly, however, he looked scared, like a kid who had been caught with his hand in the cookie jar. Carl decided to take advantage of the corporal's vulnerability.

Carl started the recorder he had brought with him. They had no video recording, but Carl wasn't concerned about that.

"Corporal Rollins, Lori Newton was murdered earlier this week, as you know. We think she was killed because of a disagreement over procuring drugs for distribution here on the base, a drug deal about which we have evidence that you are involved." Carl was stretching the truth a bit, but the corporal didn't know that.

"I know nothing about any drugs here, Lieutenant."

Carl ignored the soldier's comment and plowed ahead. "Not only that, Corporal, but we now have evidence that Captain McCain's mother did not die from an accident, but we believe she was murdered by Lori Newton."

Corporal Rollins became ashen and looked like he might pass out. Carl still didn't break stride. "Corporal, you need to know that you could be charged as an accessory to either one, or both, of these crimes since your participation in the drug activities on the base was directly related to the murders."

Corporal Rollins tried to interrupt, but Carl continued, "I am required to tell you that you may have an attorney present. If you cannot afford an attorney, one will be appointed for you." Carl completed the requisite Miranda directive and had the stricken soldier sign the disclaimer. Rollins had foolishly declined having an attorney present, and Carl proceeded.

"Corporal Rollins, you can help yourself if you tell us what you know about Lori Newton and the drug trade here on base."

Corporal Rollins had regained some of his composure. "What is in it for me if I help you?"

"We will take any murder charges against you off the table if the information you give us is credible and if you will testify if necessary."

The distraught soldier sat quietly for a few moments before he responded, "Lori Newton was a tramp and a bitch. She came on to me six months ago. I should have run right then. I mean, I thought at the time, what does this fox see in me? But the sex was good, almost addictive, so I did whatever she asked. After I gave her the names of some guys on base who I knew were in the drug scene, she then wanted information from some of the files. I refused, but she threatened to expose me and say that I raped her. I just got deeper and deeper into a mess I couldn't get out of."

"It sounds to me, Corporal, that you had a pretty strong motive to kill her," Brian interjected.

"I didn't kill her, sir. I admit I was afraid that she had something hidden away which would incriminate me, but I was in an all- night poker game until 3:00 a.m. the night she was killed, and there are five other guys who took all my money. I'm sure they will remember."

With what sounded like a rock solid alibi, Carl encouraged Rollins to continue. "Where did Lori get the drugs which she sold on base, Corporal?" Carl asked.

"She hooked up with a guy from St. Louis, Foster was his name. I remember because she laughed about his name, Faster Foster, she said. They had a falling out, however, a week or so ago. Foster wanted to stop supplying drugs for the base for awhile because you guys were putting pressure on him. Lori told me that he was a gutless wonder and that she was making what she called 'alternative arrangements' with some wetback."

"Were you present at any meetings between Lori and Foster or any other drug dealer?"

"No, Lieutenant, I swear I didn't sell drugs, I didn't use drugs, and didn't meet with anybody. All I did was follow my dick one time and I got hooked. I just gave that bitch information, that's all, and I'll take a lie detector test to prove it, if you want."

"What happened between Lori and my mother, Corporal?" Brian asked.

"When General Newton discovered that some of his pain meds were missing, Lori became really concerned. I had never seen her that upset. She always seemed to be super cool under pressure. Yeah, she would go ballistic once in a while, but it was like a volcano. Once she erupted, it was like the pressure was released and she then meticulously outlined a plan to get back on track. The deal with your mother was different, though. She was thoroughly pissed at your mom, and she came to me and demanded to look through your records and your mother's employment file. She smiled and told me that she was going to get rid of that bitch, once and for all. Sorry, Captain, but that's what she said."

"Did she say how she intended to get rid of Ms. McCain?" Carl asked.

"No, she just said that she was going to use you, Captain, to get your mother moved off base."

"So she didn't say anything about actually killing the captain's mother, just getting her moved off base?"

"That's right, Lieutenant, that's all she said that day."

"What do you mean, that day, Corporal?" Carl asked.

"Well, the day that Captain McCain's mother died, Ms. McCain had called here and asked if I knew Lori Newton's cell phone number. She said she didn't want to bother the general or his other daughter, but she wanted to speak with Lori about something."

"That was the same day my mother died?" Brian quickly interjected.

"Yes, Captain, the same day. I remember because I thought it was ironic that the next day we heard that your mother had died within a few hours of her wanting to talk with Lori, but we were told it was an accident, so I didn't think much more about it."

"Corporal, I have a very important question to ask," Carl said. "Do you have any definite knowledge as to whether Lori Newton actually spoke with, or met with, Missy McCain, the day that Ms. McCain died?"

"All I know, Lieutenant, is that two days later, I asked Lori whether Captain McCain's mother got a hold of her two days earlier. Lori appeared startled and asked me how I knew that the captain's mother had called her."

"So she admitted that Ms. McCain had called her."

"Yes, sir. She was really angry that I knew about it, and she told me that if I breathed a word of that to anyone, not only would my career be over, I may end up just like that nosy bitch. I'm sorry, Captain. I hate saying those terrible things about your mother. She was always real nice to me, but that's what Lori said. I told you, she scared the shit out of me. She was a mean person, a real mean person."

"Corporal, Lieutenant Watson and I appreciate your honesty. Obviously, you violated the trust and duties of your position, but it seems to me that you were coerced into doing things which you know were wrong. I will speak with General Newton about how to deal with this, but in the meantime you are not to speak with anyone about our conversation. Understand?"

"Yes, sir."

"You are dismissed, Corporal."

After Corporal Rollins left, Carl and Brian just looked at each other for a moment. "What do you think, Carl? Do you believe him?"

"Absolutely. He was scared shitless. Although we never could make a charge of accessory to murder stick, he didn't know that, but I think it scared him into telling the truth. I think he is just some Iowa hick who was taken in by a beautiful girl with an agenda and great tits. Not the first time that happened, and it certainly won't be the last."

"Do you think Lori went to see my mother?"

"Brian, I am convinced that your mother knew more about Lori than was safe. Your mother didn't realize it, but she was dealing with a cornered rattlesnake, and that snake bit back. Commonly, people like Lori who are addicted to their own power and greed don't even notice the common folk, if you will, like your mother, who are quietly in the background doing what Lori perceives as menial work. Your mother probably saw or heard something that threatened Lori. When Lori became a threat to her son, your mother probably tried to reason with Lori, or maybe your mother became the trapped mama bear who was going to protect her cub. In any event, I think Lori realized that the only way she could be safe from what your mother knew was to arrange for her so-called accident. Yes, in my book, Lori killed your mother."

CHAPTER THIRTY

The following morning, Mouse stormed into Carl's office like a whirling dervish. "We got the son of a bitch. We nailed him!"

"We got who, Mouse?" Carl responded.

"Faster, we got Faster for the Newton murder. Doc Boyle just called me and said that the DNA is a perfect, I mean 100 per cent perfect, match with the blood smear we got from the car. Between that and what the surveillance guys and Rollins gave us, we've got a slam dunk case, don't you think, Carl?"

Carl's mood, which had been sullen for the past couple of days, perked up dramatically. "Hell yes, we got enough to even convince that prick Jameson to take the case to the Grand Jury. Did the ME or the CSI come up with anything else, you know, like frosting on the cake?"

"Carl, we don't need frosting. We got cake, fork, plate, the whole shebang. We got that sucker nailed," Mouse replied. "But, no, they didn't find anything else of interest, except a few hairs in the back seat which they assumed were from the perp, but the DNA was different. They probably have been sitting there for a long time. They weren't pubic hairs, so probably not from a quickie that Lori had in the back seat, and they weren't Lori's. Nothing to worry about, though."

"Okay, Mouse, get in touch with Fogarty and set up a meet with Levine, Jameson's deputy, so we can fill him in on what we've got. Meanwhile, I'll bring Brian McCain up to date."

At two o'clock that afternoon, Fogarty, Mouse, and Carl were again shown into the State's Attorney's massive conference room by his trophy Executive Assistant. As she exited from the boss's private inner sanctum to greet them, she had a flushed, somewhat rumpled appearance, a far cry from the previous ice cold aloofness present at their first visit. All three of the policemen immediately had the same thought. Nothing like a quick trick on the couch— job security is wonderful, isn't it?

Aaron Levine, the Chief Deputy, was already seated in the conference room. He stood and warmly welcomed the trio. "Mr. Jameson is going to join us momentarily," he said.

Mouse, in his usual uninhibited fashion, responded, "Oh, I'm sure. Drug case, beautiful victim, death of a war hero's mother, hard on crime, a slam dunk conviction; just what the doctor ordered for the Man, right?"

Carl smiled as Levine judiciously replied, "Mr. Jameson is always pleased when excellent police work brings a hardened criminal to justice."

Mouse quietly mumbled "Bullshit," just as the Man walked briskly into the room.

"Okay, I've got an appointment in ten minutes, so fill me in on what you've got," Jameson bellowed.

After Carl related the hard evidence they had against Foster, the suspicions about the McCain killing, Corporal Rollins' testimony, and the DNA results, even Jameson had to smile.

"Sounds like a wrap," he said, and he turned to Levine. "Aaron, I want you to personally handle this case, but keep me informed. I will want to be there for your opening and closing statements, of course," and he turned and left just as abruptly as he had entered.

Mouse gazed at Jameson's departure and, after the door had been slammed closed, he turned to Levine,. "Do you believe that guy? What an asshole. How do you put up with him day after day?"

Levine merely smiled and ignored Mouse's comments. "I want you to pick Foster up, read him his rights, and charge him. You know the drill. Meanwhile, I am planning on taking the case to the Grand Jury in three or four days. That way, we can get him arraigned quickly and not have to tell the defense all of the evidence we plan to present at his trial."

Carl nodded, and the three policemen left. They got a judge to sign off on the warrant and then proceeded to Foster's condo to pick him up.

Slower Stoker was stationed at his usual spot outside Faster's private entrance. Mouse merely waved the warrant in Slower's face. "Rufus, we got a warrant. Don't even bother calling him. Just get the elevator for us."

Slower obviously had warned Faster, however, because Dewayne was casually waiting for them as they exited the private elevator at his penthouse condo.

"Dewayne Foster, you are under arrest for the murder of Lori Newton," Mouse began.

Faster's expression immediately changed from one of bored indifference to one of amazement. "Murder? What the hell are you talking about? Sure, we talked about Lori Newton being wasted, but I told you I had nothing to do with it."

"Tell it to the judge," Mouse replied, with obvious pleasure in doing so, and he proceeded to recite Miranda.

CHAPTER THIRTY—ONE

Aaron Levine was supremely confident in their case, although Faster continued to adamantly profess his innocence, his defense relying on the tried and true SODDI tactic—Some Other Dude Done It. As the convening of the Grand Jury drew nearer, Faster's characteristic swagger was rapidly fading. The reality that he was indeed in deep guano was beginning to sink in.

A Grand Jury hearing is different from the usual criminal trial in that the prosecution has a much freer rein to control the proceedings. All that Levine had to do was to convince the impaneled group that a crime had indeed occurred and that there was sufficient evidence to conclude that Faster may have been responsible for the murder of Lori Newton. As a result, Pierre Maisson got only a cursory look at the evidence against his client, and he was not allowed to present much of a defense.

After the first day of testimony, Levine felt even more assured that Faster would be held over for trial. He just had a couple of minor housekeeping items to wrap up the following day, so, for the first time in weeks, Carl felt as though he could relax somewhat. Little did he know how that would dramatically change before the day was done.

Carl had just arrived at his apartment around 5:30 after the first day of testimony, when his pager went off. He answered the call, expecting some mundane problem to deal with, and he was greeted with the bellow of Robert Jameson, the State's Attorney.

"Lieutenant, you get your dumb ass in my office now, and I mean now," and Jameson slammed the receiver down. Carl just stood there, stupefied. He had no idea what was happening, but he knew it couldn't be good.

Carl hustled downtown to Jameson's office. He remained equally puzzled and concerned as he anxiously waited for Jameson to appear.

After about ten minutes, the State's Attorney and his Chief Deputy appeared together. To Carl's surprise, Fogarty sheepishly followed, looking like the delinquent kid who had just been taken to the woodshed. Jameson's face was beet red with anger, while Levine was a picture of contrast, his ashen face appearing as though he had seen a ghost.

Before Carl could say a word, Jameson laid into him. "Lieutenant, what kind of dumb shits are you and Fogarty? You two so-called detectives act more like Keystone Kops than real policemen. I should take both of your shields. You have made this office look like we don't have a clue what in the hell we are doing, and I don't like having egg on my face, especially when it's due to incompetence of bumbling idiots like the two of you."

"Sir, I don't know what you are talking about," Carl interjected.

"No shit, you don't know what I am talking about, Lieutenant. You don't even know what your own men are doing. Fogarty, fill the eminent detective in on the latest catastrophe."

Fogarty apologetically explained. "Carl, remember how we had Foster under surveillance and the two policemen we had shadowing him overheard the argument between Lori Newton and him?"

"Sure I remember. Was there something wrong with their testimony?"

"That's the deal. They didn't testify today because they have been out of town for a week taking a prisoner to Idaho for an outstanding warrant out West, and they then were on vacation, hunting in the mountains until they got back later this afternoon. Their testimony was relayed via an affidavit, so they have been out of touch since the morning after Lori Newton was killed."

"I still don't understand," Carl said. "Their testimony was still good."

"Yeah, their testimony was good," Fogarty explained, "but the night that Lori was killed, they had decided to keep an eye on Faster, trying to get more evidence on the drug case. They were watching his place from 7:00 that night, when they saw him come in, until well after 2:30 in the morning, when the lights went off in Faster's place. Carl, there was no way he could have left that condo without those guys seeing him. He couldn't have killed Lori. Two St. Louis police officers are his alibi, and you don't get much more solid than that. We just found out about all this an hour ago when they heard that we had made Faster for killing Lori."

Carl slumped into a nearby chair, sweat pouring from his forehead. "Oh, Christ, now we are back at square one. Who in the hell killed Lori Newton?"

CHAPTER THIRTY—TWO

Faster Foster was released that night with a smug I-told-you-so grin on his face as he climbed into Pierre Maisson's pimp-mobile and merrily waved as he drove off.

The following day, Carl assembled the troops, Mouse, Fogarty, Dr. Boyle, the ME, and the CSI techies. The doctor and lab guys remained adamantly convinced that the DNA in Lori Newton's car matched that of Faster Foster. They admitted they had compared the blood smear taken at the scene only with the single comparator which came from the tissue Faster Foster had so conveniently provided, not with any other DNA samples. Although there was not yet a universal computer data bank housing DNA on anyone who had ever been arrested, in the military, or employed by the government, there were some limited such programs available.

Carl told them, "I want you to go back and recheck the test, and you need to do DNA analysis on that extraneous hair found in Lori Newton's back seat, and compare that with everybody, and I mean everybody, who had anything even remotely related to Lori Newton. We can't require anyone to give us a sample, but if anyone refuses, it's going to make me really suspicious. Tell them that we need the specimen to eliminate them as leaving trace evidence so we can concentrate on the others. Maybe that will placate them."

"Carl, that's a lot of people," Dr. Boyle complained.

"Doc, somehow we screwed this deal up, so we need to do whatever it takes to make it right. I'll tell you what. We'll start with General Newton, his daughter, Kaitlyn, Brian McCain, Corporal Rollins, Slower Stoker, Ricardo Castillo, and that goon who works for him," Carl responded.

"You don't really think that General Newton, his daughter, or Brian McCain killed Lori, do you?" Mouse asked.

"No, I don't," Carl replied. "I still think somehow Foster snuck out without those two cops seeing him and did her, but we can't afford not to turn over every single rock. Otherwise, all of us will be out pounding a beat if Jameson has his way."

Over the next week, Carl, Mouse, and Fogarty got specimens for DNA comparison from everyone Carl had identified, with the exception of Castillo and his henchman, which was not surprising. Carl had just thrown their names into the mix for completeness, but he really didn't think any of the people he had named were going to come up as a match.

Finally, the following Thursday, Dr. Boyle called Carl. "Carl, I need to come over and talk to you."

"What is it, Doc? Do you have a match for us?"

"It'll make more sense if I could explain it to you. Get Fogarty and Mouse and I'll be at your office in 45 minutes."

Once again, Carl had to wait anxiously, since it was obvious that the good doctor had something to share with them. When the ME finally arrived, he sat down and began to explain.

"Okay, I have good news and I have bad news. First, the hair samples in the backseat had the follicle attached, so we were able to do DNA testing, and it didn't match any of the specimens you got for us.

"Secondly," he continued, "we rechecked the original blood smear and the DNA definitely matched Dewayne Foster."

"So we were right, after all!" Mouse exclaimed. "He must have snuck out and killed Lori."

"Please, Mouse, let me continue. The blood smear also matched another of the specimens you supplied, that of Brian McCain."

"But that's impossible, Doc," Carl said. "You've testified time and again that DNA is unique to an individual, and if there is an unequivocal match, it has to be one and the same."

"That's right, Carl. I have testified to that fact many times, but there is one exception—if the two samples come from identical twins."

There was an uncomprehending silence in the room. "Are you telling me that Dewayne Foster and Brian McCain are identical twins and that Brian may have been the one in the back seat of that car?" Carl asked, incredulously.

"That's exactly what I'm saying," he replied.

"Jesus Christ!" Mouse exclaimed. "They don't look anything alike. How could they be identical twins?"

Carl leaned back in his chair, overwhelmed with this new information. "Think about it, Mouse. Faster is a long time drug abuser with a big time cocaine habit. He's lost a ton of weight. He's a scrawny dude with a big Afro. Brian, on the other hand is a physically fit hunk, but if you look at their bone structure, I could envision how they could indeed be identical twins. As much as I hate to say it, Mouse, bring Brian McCain in. We need to talk with him."

86

CHAPTER THIRTY—THREE

Carl was sick, not physically sick, but devastated by the turn of events. He knew that Brian McCain could not have killed Lori Newton. He was still convinced that Faster Foster should be their focus, but after he had personally interviewed the cops who had Foster under surveillance, even Carl began to doubt whether they would ever be able to shake the policemen's testimony. They were absolutely sure that Faster Foster never left his condo before they left at 2:30 in the morning.

When Mouse and Fogarty escorted Brian McCain into his office, Carl's first thought was that Brian looked even worse than Carl felt. The captain's usually immaculate uniform was wrinkled and unkempt. He hadn't shaved, and he looked as though he hadn't slept for a week.

"Captain, how much has Sergeant Brannon explained to you as to the most recent developments?" Carl began.

"Only that Foster was released because of new evidence, but I knew that several days ago. That's all that I know."

"Captain, I am required to read you the Miranda warning," Carl began, as he simultaneously turned on the recorder sitting off to the side of his desk.

"No need, Lieutenant. I am familiar with my rights, but why do you need to Mirandize me?" Nonetheless, Carl proceeded with the formality, just to make sure that everything was done according to the letter of the law.

The two men, who had developed a sense of mutual respect if not outright friendship during the past several weeks, now adopted a tenor of formality, since they both realized that things had changed dramatically over the past five minutes.

"Captain McCain, as you know, we have irrefutable evidence from two police officers who had Faster Foster under surveillance that Mr. Foster could not have killed Lori Newton because he never left his penthouse the night of the murder. As a result, the ME went back and compared trace evidence found in Miss Newton's car with comparative specimens voluntarily provided by you and others who may have been in the decedent's car, the purpose being to eliminate those people as being the source of some hair we found in the car, for example."

"I understand, Lieutenant, but I still don't know what that has to do with me."

"Captain, you know that we found a blood smear in Lori Newton's car, a smear that suggests it came from her assailant, since it was found on the back of the driver side headrest, where her attacker apparently was when he strangled her."

"Yes, I know that, Captain, and I know the smear matched Faster Foster, so why is he not still in custody?"

"He was released because of the police officers' testimony, as I explained," Carl replied. "Captain, DNA analysis of that blood was a perfect match to Faster Foster, but it was also a perfect match to your DNA. Do you understand what I am saying?"

"No, Captain, I don't understand. How could the one sample belong to both Faster Foster and to me?"

"Because Faster Foster is your identical twin, Captain. He is your brother."

Brian McCain was dumbfounded. He leaned back in his chair and stared at Carl. "What do you mean, my identical twin? Does he know that we are related, if we really are related? Did my mother know that she had twins and, if so, did she just walk away and leave one behind? Did she know that her other son was a no good drug dealer and probably a murderer?"

"Brian," Carl interjected, with a much more conciliatory tone, "I'm sure you have lots of questions, so do we, but the most immediate thing I need to know is whether you have ever been in Lori Newton's car?"

"Lieutenant, I was a passenger in her car one time, and one time only. About two months ago, my car was in the shop, and Lori gave me a ride to pick it up after the repairs were done, but I was in the passenger seat. I have never driven her car, and I certainly have never been in the back seat."

"Where were you the night that Lori Newton was killed?" Sergeant Fogarty asked.

"I was home alone, in bed, all night, and no, I don't have anyone who can confirm that. No visitors, no phone calls, nothing. But surely you don't think I killed Lori. Why would I want her dead?"

Immediately after he asked the rhetorical question, Brian McCain realized what he had asked. Of course he had a reason to want her dead. After all, Lori Newton had threatened to destroy his career, to accuse him of rape. Even more devastating was the fact that it was now common knowledge that Lori Newton was responsible for his mother getting fired. The final nail in the motive coffin was that Lori Newton had undoubtedly killed his mother, and

88

Brian McCain was privy to all the evidence of that crime.

The room was deadly silent, for everyone present was thinking exactly the same thing that Brian McCain had recognized. He had motive and opportunity, and there was strong evidence against him. Brian slumped forward, his head in his hands. Then he slowly raised his head, looked Carl squarely in the eye, and said, "I think I need an attorney."

CHAPTER THIRTY—FOUR

The interrogation of Brian McCain was put in abeyance until his attorney, Peter Scott, arrived an hour later. The attorney was the antithesis of Pierre Maisson. Peter Scott was a conservative, middle aged, sober counselor who was well respected in the St. Louis legal community. He met privately with his client after Carl had filled him in on the facts of the case. Carl indicated that Brian was not under arrest at this time, but he remained a "person of interest." As a result, Mr. Scott advised his client not to answer any additional questions, and the twosome departed.

Brian had asked many of the questions which had plagued Carl and Mouse. Carl dispatched Mouse to try to trace down any records from the old City Hospital, while Carl returned to Faster Foster's condo.

When Carl entered the plush living room, he again pondered, as he had many times before, how the old dictum that "Crime doesn't pay" was a bunch of hogwash. Some of the guys that Carl had put away over the years had digs which made Carl's humble apartment look almost decrepit.

"What can I do for you Lieutenant Watson?" Faster asked, with a wry smile on his face. Carl noted that Faster was looking more emaciated every time he saw him, and his nose bleeds were now nearly continuous.

Carl proceeded to explain to Foster about the DNA findings indicating that he had an identical twin, although Carl didn't elaborate by telling him who his twin and his mother were. Faster was neither particularly surprised nor concerned about the unexpected news.

"Interesting," was all he said. "I was left in the hospital by my mother, no name, no family, just a nobody," he said. "My name was given to me in the first foster home where I was placed. I lived with the Foster family for about 4 years, when they were put away for dealing drugs. They just wanted me so they could get a monthly check from the state for taking in a foster child."

"Do you know what your birth date was, Faster?" Carl asked.

"Yeah, it was June 28, 1972. Why?"

"Just curious," Carl replied, but he didn't tell him that it was the same birth date as Brian McCain. "So you never knew who your birth mother or father were, and you didn't know of any brothers or sisters, right?"

"That's right. Born a street kid, raised a street kid, and I'll probably die on the street, you know Lieutenant. Kind of interesting. So I got a brother, huh, and an identical twin at that. I may have to look him up some day."

Carl got up to leave, but as he walked toward the door, he turned to the sick-looking man and said, "You know, Faster, you should get that nose bleed checked out. It looks like it's getting a lot worse," and the cop headed for the elevator.

When Carl got back to the office, Mouse had just returned from trying to retrieve any old records from the Obstetrics ward at City Hospital in 1972, but the records for June were lost.

"I figured it would be too easy to find those records," Mouse complained, "but we still know that Faster and Brian are Missy McCain's kids."

"I called Brian while you were gone," Carl explained to Mouse. "He said that his mother never said anything about having twins, but he does know that she had a Cesarean section, which is commonly done for multiple births, but that doesn't prove anything. The other curious thing he told me was that every year on his birthday his mother would get very somber and say to him, 'Brian, we need to pray for you and for anybody out there who is like you.' He thought she was just speaking in generalities, but now he wonders if there was more meaning to that comment, especially since she repeated the same year after year."

CHAPTER THIRTY—FIVE

After the policeman left his condo, Faster had a moment of introspection, which was decidedly unusual for this self professed "man of the street." Faster had recently been experiencing increasing anxiety about whether he might have something seriously wrong. He had continued to lose weight and he was having fevers and violent shaking chills nearly daily for the past 3-4 days, to say nothing of the now continuous dripping of fresh blood from his nose and from his swollen gums. He had become so weak, probably from the blood loss, he suspected, that he nearly passed out whenever he stood up quickly.

Faster pulled out his cell phone and looked up the number of the doctor he called only on those rare occasions when he felt sick. Dewayne Foster was not what any physician would call a" compliant patient." He took lousy care of himself and had no concept of preventative care, but old Dr. Amos Blevins, his family doctor, cared for many others in the black part of St. Louis who were the same, so he just patched his patients up as best he could and sent them back to their lousy life styles.

When Faster explained his symptoms to Dr. Blevins' nurse, she recognized that this might be a serious problem, so she put him on hold and spoke with the doctor. She got back on the line and told Faster to come into the office in an hour. They would do some blood tests and the doctor would see him right after that.

Faster was becoming more and more alarmed, especially since he could sense the concern in the nurse's voice, so he presented himself as instructed. It was ironic that Faster, who was a long time drug addict, had never used IV drugs in his life. In fact, he was petrified about being poked with a needle of any kind. Nonetheless, he grimaced and reluctantly allowed the lab technician to draw three tubes of blood that Dr. Blevins had ordered, a blue top tube, a purple top tube, and a striped red top tube. The tech had to use an adhesive wrap bandage to keep the needle puncture site from bleeding, and Faster was then shown into a small sterile-looking examination room. The nurse checked his temperature, pulse, and blood pressure, and she then took a more complete medical history from him. She curtly told Faster that the doctor would be in to see him "shortly", after the lab results were back, but Faster knew that "shortly" would probably be at least an hour.

Faster was wrong. It was an hour and a half before the kindly old black physician entered the room, a look of concern clearly etched on his weathered face.

Dr. Blevins was a busy man, and he never wasted time on niceties or formalities. He came straight to the point.

"Dewayne, your blood tests show that you are not making enough good platelets, which are necessary to stop bleeding, or white blood cells, which help fight infection."

"What does that mean, Doc?"

"What it means, Dewayne, is that you have acute leukemia, and you need treatment right away. I've already made arrangements for you to be admitted to Barnes Hospital. Dr. Lisa O'Malley is an excellent hematologist, and she will get you started on treatment immediately."

"Wait a minute, Doc. Slow down. Leukemia—isn't that a kind of cancer? And I got things to do; I can't go to some damn hospital right away. And I'm not going to have some broad take care of me. I need to think about this."

"Dewayne, listen to me," Dr. Blevins calmly replied. He now sat down across a small table from Faster. His tone had softened dramatically as he recognized that this was a sentinel event for his patient, one that needed careful and thorough explanation.

"Dewayne, my boy, let me explain this to you. The bone marrow normally makes red blood cells, white blood cells, and platelets, but your bone marrow is not functioning normally. It is not making enough red blood cells, so you are anemic. That is why you get tired so easily. It is also not making enough platelets, so your blood won't clot normally. That is why you have had nose bleeds, bleeding from your gums, and bruising. Most importantly, it is not making normal white blood cells, so you are susceptible to infections, and these infections can be life threatening. That is why it is so important to get you into the hospital as soon as possible—today—so they can start treatment. The abnormal white blood cells your bone marrow is making are overrunning the normal blood cells."

Dr. Blevins continued. "As to Dr. O'Malley, she is one of the foremost experts in the area in dealing with acute leukemia. I have the utmost respect for her abilities. In fact, I have sent family members to see her for consultation."

Faster stared absently at the wall, absolutely stunned. He then turned to Dr. Blevins and quietly said, "Okay, tell me what I need to do."

93

The next several days were a blur to Dewayne Foster. Dr. Blevins wouldn't even let him drive alone to Barnes Hospital, the primary teaching hospital for the Washington University Medical School. Faster called Slower, who got a friend to drive Faster's car back to the condo while Slower delivered Dewayne to Dr. O'Malley's office. She turned out to be a delightful, very attractive African American lady with a real "take charge" demeanor. Faster liked her immediately, primarily because she was obviously very knowledgeable, but also because she was from what Faster perceived as the "old school." She had that unique ability to make her patients feel confident and comfortable, even in the face of a life threatening disease.

Faster was admitted to the hospital and immediately had a bone marrow test. He was then given transfusions of both red blood cells and platelets after numerous additional tubes of blood were drawn. As Dr. O'Malley examined him, Faster remarked to her, "Doc, no wonder I have no blood. You guys have taken it all, and then you turn around and give me someone else's."

"I'm sure it seems like that, Dewayne, but we need to do lots of special tests, like DNA testing, in case you might need a bone marrow transplant, or more likely a stem cell transplant, which is kind of the same, but a lot easier on both you and the donor."

"Oh, I know all about DNA testing, Doc," Faster responded.

Dr. O'Malley stopped what she was doing, surprised at Faster's knowledge of DNA. "What do you mean you know about DNA testing, Dewayne?"

Faster was embarrassed to explain all about his history with the police, Lori Newton, and his learning that he had an identical twin, all within the past week, but he told the doctor what had transpired.

"Do you mean to tell me that you have an identical twin, Dewayne?" Dr. O'Malley asked, incredulous at this stroke of good fortune.

"Sure. That's what the cop told me."

She peppered Faster with questions. "Who is this twin? Where does he live? Is he healthy? Is he willing to donate stem cells for you if needed?"

"Slow down, Doc. I don't know who it is. Maybe the cops or the ME know, but they never told me. What's the big deal anyway? I've never even met the guy."

"Dewayne, the big deal is that this stranger, who also happens to be your identical twin, could save your life."

The doctors had placed a device called a port under the skin of Faster's chest so they could easily give him antibiotics and blood transfusions. They

94

could also use it to draw the numerous blood samples they needed to monitor his status.

Dr. O'Malley had been brutally honest when she described the side effects of the "drug cocktail" that she was going to give him, and her description was unfortunately right on. Faster had taken some bad cocaine over the years, but nothing compared to how crappy he felt from the chemotherapy. In fact, more than once he had told the doctor, "I don't want this chemo anymore. Just stop it. I'd rather die than go through this." She encouraged and cajoled him through the five days of chemo, complete with unrelenting nausea and vomiting, although the nurses gave him medications which helped out with the side effects. Mostly, though, Faster was fortunately out of it enough from the high fevers, which eventually subsided as the antibiotics took over, that he was oblivious to much of what went on.

For most of his nearly four week hospitalization, Dewayne was in isolation, where the nurses, doctors, and even the few visitors who came by had to wear masks, gloves, and gowns so they didn't introduce further infections to his ravaged body. Finally, when his blood counts began to rise on their own, Dr. O'Malley was able to enter his room without all the protective paraphernalia.

"Dewayne, you have reached the first milestone. No more isolation."

"Thank God, Doc, although I'm not sure even God would want to go through what you just put me through. Does that mean that I'm cured? When do I get to go home?" he asked excitedly.

"It won't be long now, Dewayne, before we will be able to discharge you. After that, though, you will need to come back into the hospital for a shorter course of what we call consolidation chemotherapy, assuming that another bone marrow test shows that you are in complete remission. That will be fewer days of chemo, and since your bone marrow will hopefully be normal, you won't be nearly as sick as you were the first time. After that, though, we need to consider a stem cell transplant. That would greatly increase the odds of your remaining in complete remission for a long time, perhaps even a cure. Do you remember us talking about that at the very beginning?"

"Yeah, I remember, Doc. But don't we need to find out about my twin if we are going to do that?"

"Yes, that would be preferable. Although we commonly use an unrelated donor for stem cell transplants, using an identical twin wouldmake it much less risky and more likely to be effective. I will be following up with trying to find out who your twin is, if the authorities even know."

CHAPTER THIRTY—SIX

During the month that Dewayne Foster was languishing in the hospital, Carl Watson and his team had not been idle. They knew it would be very difficult to pin Lori Newton's murder on Dewayne Foster, but Carl was determined to prove that Brian McCain was not involved.

Several days after Brian was questioned, Carl received a phone call from Lori's father, of all people.

"Lieutenant, this is General Newton."

"Yes, sir," Carl replied.

"Lieutenant, I loved my daughter, but I am also a realist. She was not a nice person. In fact, she was an evil person. Lieutenant, I would not wish my daughter dead, but I have done my grieving. I cannot believe that Brian had anything to do with her death. Brian is like a son to me, and, Lieutenant, I would do anything I can to help prove that he is innocent. Do you understand me?"

"Yes, sir."

"If there is anything that Brian needs—money, lawyers, anything—I am going to provide it."

"I understand sir," Carl again replied, and the General abruptly hung up.

A policeman's job is usually to look for evidence to help convict the perpetrator, but Mouse and Carl had spoken with Brian several times, trying to get evidence which would prove his innocence. Brian still insisted he was home alone, with no alibi for the night in question. Just to close the loop, however, Mouse checked the log book which the sentries at Fort Leonard Wood used to monitor all traffic onto and off the base. Since Brian had no family, he lived in the BOQ, Bachelor Officer's Quarters, on the base. On the night that Lori Newton was killed, a car with Brian's license plate number left the base at midnight and didn't return until nearly 2:00 a.m.

Mouse took this incriminating evidence back to Carl. They were feeling more betrayed by the minute. Not only had Brian been off base when Lori was killed, he compounded it by lying to them as to his whereabouts.

The policemen drove down to the base to confront Brian with this new evidence. They again read him his rights before asking again where he was the night Lori was killed. Brian looked to them like a picture of defeat.

"Lieutenant, I wasn't entirely truthful about my whereabouts that night. I was so upset about my mother's death and Lori's possible involvement that I just couldn't sleep. I was beside myself with worry about how this would affect the General and Kate. Do you remember when you talked about unintended consequences? That was all I could think about—how the fallout would impact all the people who Lori betrayed during her life. Anyway, I got up and drove around for a few hours, just trying to decide what to do next. I don't even know where I drove. I just wanted to get away and try to clear my head."

"Why did you lie to us?" Carl asked.

"I knew that it sounded like a lame excuse, and I thought it would incriminate me even more if I admitted I had left the base. I am so used to the sentries that I completely forgot that they would have a record of me leaving. You must believe me, that's the truth."

Carl and Mouse didn't respond. They merely nodded and left. There really was nothing they could say to Brian which would make him feel better.

On the return trip to the office, Mouse said, "Well, I think that's that. Brian McCain is screwed. He must have done it. He admits that he had a motive to kill Lori, and now we know he had the opportunity to do so, and he has no alibi. It's too bad. I liked the guy, and Lori Newton certainly deserved dying. You talk about unintended consequences; look at poor Brian McCain and what she ended up doing to him."

Carl was eerily quiet, and he solemnly responded, "Mouse, you have no idea, no idea at all."

Mouse turned and looked at his partner, confused about the lieutenant's comment.

CHAPTER THIRTY-- SEVEN

Carl called and made an appointment to meet with Aaron Levine, Jameson's Chief Deputy in the State's Attorney office. Mouse, Fogarty, and he laid out the evidence they had accumulated implicating Brian McCain in the death of Lori Newton. Levine listened attentively, and then responded, "You guys screwed this up once. I hope to God you've got it right this time. I'm going to run this by Mr. Jameson. Wait here," and he left the room. Fogarty and Mouse had done most of the talking with Levine. Carl was still strangely quiet, as he had been since they left the base.

Robert Jameson barged into the room. "Levine told me what you have found out. If you hadn't fucked up this case with Foster, I would think this new evidence would be a slam dunk, but you guys make me nervous. Are you sure about what you've got?"

Carl interrupted, "Mr. Jameson, if you don't think you have the evidence to convict Brian McCain, why don't you just let him go, and we can dig deeper."

Fogarty and Mouse stared at Carl. They knew that there were no more rocks out there for them to turn over. If they were going to get a conviction for the murder of Lori Newton, it had to be with the evidence they now had.

Jameson was irate. "The press is all over this case. It doesn't sit well with the voters if a pretty blond woman, who happens to be the daughter of an army general, is killed in the middle of Forest Park. It doesn't instill a lot of confidence in the police department or my office if we don't aggressively punish the perpetrator."

"Even if the victim is a drug dealer and possible murderer herself," Carl replied. "And if the victim had been a black woman killed on Delmar at one in the morning, it wouldn't have been as important, is that what you are saying?"

"Watch yourself, Lieutenant. You are treading on thin ice. You know that's not what I meant, and I better never hear otherwise. Do you understand?"

Jameson then turned to his deputy. "Aaron, forget about the Grand Jury. Let's take this case directly to Superior Court for an indictment. Ask for no bail, but I'm sure the court will let him out," and he strode from the room.

"You heard him, Lieutenant. Pick Brian McCain up and charge him with second degree murder.

CHAPTER THIRTY—EIGHT

Over the next two weeks, Brian had been arraigned and, as expected, been granted bail at $1 million, which meant that he had to come up with $100,000. General Newton, as he had promised, provided the funds to allow Brian to at least return to his home for the time being. Peter Scott, his attorney, had decided to push ahead with a speedy trial, his thinking being that there was no advantage to his client to drag the proceedings out. By the end of the month, the jury had been impaneled and the trial had begun.

The prosecution opened by presenting the scientific evidence, including the supposition that Lori had been garroted from behind, with the assailant in the back seat. Aaron Levine was interviewing Dr. Boyle, the Medical Examiner.

"Could the person who attacked Miss Newton have done so from any position other than from behind her, in the back seat, Doctor?"

"Based upon the autopsy findings which showed the brunt of the force from the strangulation was on the larynx and hyoid bone, with less direct trauma posteriorly, it is my opinion that the assailant had to have approached the victim from behind."

"That being said, Doctor, isn't it likely that the assailant's face would have abutted the back side of the driver's side head rest as he strangled the victim?"

"Objection, Your Honor," the defendant's attorney said, rising gracefully from his chair. "The prosecution has not presented any evidence that the perpetrator of this crime was a 'he' rather than a 'she.' Moreover, the question calls for a conclusion from the witness."

"Mr. Scott, I am quite sure that the prosecution will be presenting evidence as to his view of the gender of the assailant. In addition, this court is fully cognizant of the importance of gender recognition and identification, but we are not going to split hairs by requiring Mr. Levine, or you for that matter, to explicitly state 'he'or 'she' every time gender is mentioned. Do I make myself clear?"

"Yes, Your Honor."

"With respect to drawing a conclusion from the witness," the jurist continued, "Dr. Boyle's credentials have been agreed upon by you. He is an expert in criminal forensics, so I will allow the question. You may proceed, Mr. Levine."

"Thank you, Your Honor. Dr. Boyle, you may answer the question."

"Yes, it is likely that the assailant would have been facing forward from the rear seat of the vehicle, so his face may have approached the head rest."

The prosecution then got into the murky subject of the DNA testing. Prior to the trial, the defense had tried to exclude the DNA as being admissible evidence since the specimen had been obtained from Brian under "false pretenses." The court, however, ruled that since Brian had signed a waiver, the DNA was therefore admissible.

"Doctor," Levine continued, "would you please explain what you found on the rear of the driver's side head rest, right where you testified it is likely that the assailant's face may have rubbed."

"The police found a smear of what we later determined was human blood."

"Was the blood that of the decedent?"

"No, it was not."

"Did you later determine whom that blood belonged to?"

"Objection, Your Honor," Peter Scott interjected. "The prosecution knows very well that Dr. Boyle cannot honestly answer that question, since the blood may have come from two different people."

Carl, who was watching the proceedings with interest, quickly glanced at the jury. Each of the twelve looked confused.

"Mr. Scott, hold your horses. Mr. Levine, do you intend to clarify this for the benefit of the court and the jury?"

"I do, Your Honor."

"Then do so."

"Doctor Boyle," Levine continued, "were you able to match the DNA from the blood smear found on the head rest in Lori Newton's car with any individual?"

"Actually, Mr. Levine, we matched it with two individuals."

"For the benefit of the court, Doctor, how could that be? Isn't it true that an exact DNA match is virtually 100% proof of the identity if there is a match between two comparative samples, such as we have in this case?"

"Normally, that is true, Mr. Levine, but in this case we are dealing with two people who are identical twins, so their DNA profiles are identical."

"So the defendant has an identical twin, and either of them could have left that blood smear at the murder scene."

100

"That is correct," Dr. Boyle responded.

"If it please the court," the prosecutor said. "The prosecution will in due course present evidence that effectively eliminates the defendant's twin as the perpetrator of this crime."

"Doctor, I would now like to address the findings related to the death of the defendant's mother, Ms. Missy McCain."

The defense attorney immediately jumped to his feet. "Your Honor, this line of questioning is uncalled for. The death of his mother has no bearing on this case."

"Your Honor," Levine rebutted, "the murder of…"

"Your Honor," Scott nearly yelled. "I insist we discuss this subject in your chambers."

The judge firmly rapped his gavel on its stand. "Both of you be silent. Mr. Scott, you are in no position to insist anything. This is my courtroom and I will make the decisions, do you understand?"

"My apologies, Your Honor, but the prosecution is offering information which is highly prejudicial to my client and which I would ask the court to rule upon before any further damage is done."

The judge and the two attorneys, as well as the court reporter, withdrew to the judge's chambers. The prosecution argued that the murder of the defendant's mother would go to motive, but the defense countered with the argument that the death certificate indicated that her death was accidental and that at this point it was pure conjecture as to the cause of death and even more conjecture as to the role, if any, that Lori Newton had in her death. After rather heated off the record discussion, the judge ruled that further mention of the death of Missy McCain would be inadmissible.

The judge and the attorneys returned to the courtroom, and after additional rather mundane forensic housekeeping items, Mr. Levine turned to the defendant's table and said, "Your witness, Counselor."

"Doctor Boyle," Peter Scott began, "I want to focus on the DNA evidence."

"I thought you might," the doctor replied, a smile on his face. Even the jury and the judge smiled at this retort.

"Doctor, is it not true that the police initially brought you a comparative specimen from a gentleman by the name of Dewayne Foster, also known on the street among his companion drug dealers as Faster Foster?'

The prosecutor shot to his feet. "Your Honor, this is material which has not yet been introduced into evidence. Therefore, it is improper cross examination. Moreover, I object to the defense referring to Mr. Foster as a drug dealer. That certainly is prejudicial and misleading."

"Mr. Levine, you opened the door for the defense to address any and all ramifications of the DNA evidence, so the defense is allowed to pursue that subject. Mr. Scott, you will refrain from making any subjective comments about any of the participants in this case, understood?"

"Yes, Your Honor. I apologize for any perceived transgression," Scott responded, knowing full well that he had achieved his ulterior motive of tainting Faster Foster in the minds of the jury.

Doctor, we were discussing your comparing the blood specimen found at the scene with that of Mr. Foster. What were your findings?"

"We found there was a perfect match."

"Therefore, Doctor, did you not surmise that Mr. Foster was present in the back seat of the victim's car?"

"Objection, Your Honor. The doctor can testify only as to the laboratory findings. Anything else would be supposition on his part."

"Objection sustained. Mr. Scott, rephrase your question."

"Thank you, Your Honor. Doctor, since there was a perfect match between the specimen in the car and that from Mr. Foster, what did you do next?'

"We notified the appropriate authorities, and they proceeded accordingly."

"Just to be sure we all understand, Doctor, is it your testimony that the specimen found in the car of Lori Newton was identical to that of Mr. Dewayne Foster? A yes or no answer would be fine."

"Yes."

"No further questions," the attorney quietly stated, as he turned to the jury, offered them a satisfied smile, and sat down.

The prosecution then called Sergeant Nolan, the senior member of the surveillance team watching Faster Foster. Nolan testified that he and Officer Symington had Dewayne Foster under surveillance from 7:00 p.m. to 2:30 a.m. the night of the murder, and at no time did they see him leave his building.

When given the opportunity to cross examine the witness, Mr. Scott asked, "Sergeant Nolan, is it not true that you and Officer Symington also had Mr. Foster under surveillance on July 3rd?"

"Objection, Your Honor. This covers matters not addressed during my direct examination of this witness."

102

"Your Honor," Scott rebutted, "the prosecution did ask about the surveillance of Mr. Foster, so I should be allowed to ask about the entire surveillance."

"Objection overruled."

The defense then had Sergeant Nolan describe the disagreement between Lori Newton and Dewayne Foster on July 3rd.

"Sergeant, it is not true that the argument between the decedent and Mr. Foster was quite heated?"

"Yes, sir. They were cussing and swearing at each other."

"Did they separate on friendly terms?"

"Not at all. They were really mad at each other when the decedent sped off."

Mr. Scott surprisingly did not question the policeman about their surveillance the night of the murder, instead electing to address this during the presentation of his own case.

Sergeant Nolan was dismissed, and the prosecution called Carl to the stand.

Carl strode to the front of the courtroom, was sworn in, and settled as comfortably as he could in the witness chair. Some policemen relished being in the spotlight as a witness, but Carl always found it intimidating. He was especially uncomfortable in this case because he was determined to try to help Brian's case, if at all possible. He had already decided that the only way to get through the ordeal would be to simply state the facts and studiously avoid offering any interpretation which might harm Brian's case, unless asked.

The prosecutor went through the usual formalities, outlining Carl's qualifications, his notification of the crime, and his arrival on the scene.

"Lieutenant, let's get right to the meat of the matter. Dr. Boyle testified that he found a perfect match between the specimen found in the victim's car and that supplied by your office, reportedly obtained from Mr. Dewayne Foster. First, how were you able to obtain a specimen from Mr. Foster? Was it voluntarily provided by him or did you have a court order to do so?"

"Neither, Mr. Levine. We were interrogating Mr. Foster, in the presence of his attorney, and they had signed a waiver agreeing that anything he said or did could be used against him. Mr. Foster had a bloody nose, and he had disposed of several bloodied tissues into the waste basket in the interview room. We took those to the ME's office for comparison."

"Lieutenant, what did you do when Dr. Boyle informed you as to the match with Mr. Foster's bloody tissue?"

"We picked Mr. Foster up."

"But Lieutenant, Mr. Foster was subsequently released. Why was that?"

"We later learned that Mr. Foster had been under surveillance by the St. Louis City Police for a separate incident. During the time of the attack on the victim, Mr. Foster was reportedly at his home."

"Thank you, Lieutenant. That seems to clear up that point of contention. When you were informed of this discrepancy, Lieutenant, what did you do next?"

"We released Mr. Foster and obtained voluntary samples from other people who may have been in the decedent's vehicle. We also found a hair in the back seat, and we wanted to eliminate others as potentially contaminating the scene."

"Is it not true, Lieutenant, that you had an unexpected bonus after you did this additional testing?

"Objection, Your Honor. The prosecutor's use of the term 'bonus' is inappropriate and prejudicial."

"Sustained."

"Lieutenant, Dr. Boyle has testified that he unexpectedly found an additional match between the specimen in the car and that supplied by the defendant, Brian McCain. Is that correct?"

"That is correct."

"Furthermore, Dr. Boyle has testified that this testing confirms that the defendant, Brian McCain, and Mr. Dewayne Foster are indeed identical twins. Is that correct?"

"Yes, sir."

"Lieutenant, as far as you are aware, did either the defendant or Mr. Foster know that he had a living identical twin?"

"To my knowledge, neither of them was aware of this, based upon the surprise they both exhibited upon being so informed."

"Moving to a different subject, Lieutenant, are you aware of any connection between the defendant and Mr. Foster prior to the murder of Lori Newton?"

"Captain McCain had asked us to help in the investigation of a possible connection between the decedent and Mr. Foster in regard to an apparent influx of drugs on the grounds of Fort Leonard Wood, where Captain McCain was based and where Miss Newton lived, but, to my knowledge, the defendant and Mr. Foster did not know each other."

" Lieutenant, is it not true that the defendant was actually raised in the

104

home of Lori Newton's father, the commanding officer at Fort Leonard Wood, where his mother was employed as a maid and nanny? In fact, the defendant and the decedent were basically raised almost as brother and sister. Is that not correct?"

"That is correct."

"Lieutenant, were you ever able to confirm a connection between the decedent and Mr. Foster?"

"We had substantial evidence that Mr. Foster was supplying drugs to Lori Newton, who then used a network which she had developed on the base to distribute the drugs."

"Lieutenant, was the defendant aware of this evidence?"

"He was. Since he had asked us to cooperate in leading the investigation, we thought it only appropriate to keep him apprised of the developments in the case."

"How did the defendant react when you told him of the decedent's role in the drug trafficking at Fort Leonard Wood? After all, such a conspiracy, when it became public, would effectively derail the career of General Newton, the man who had effectively raised him, and a man who the defendant greatly admired."

"Objection, Your Honor. The prosecution is editorializing. Is there a question for the witness buried in that soliloquy?"

"Sustained. Mr. Levine, please refrain from sermonizing, and I don't intend to tell you again."

"My apologies to the court, Your Honor.

"What did the defendant say when you informed him of the evidence against Lori Newton, Lieutenant?"

"He was not at all pleased."

Aaron Levine looked fixedly at Carl and said, "I suspect not at all pleased would be an understatement, Lieutenant, but let's move along. Lieutenant, the defendant's mother worked in the Newton household for many years, yet she rather suddenly moved away. Do you know what caused this rather sudden change in living arrangements?"

"We were initially told by General Newton that some pain medications which he kept on hand for flare up of a chronic back condition were missing and that his daughter, Lori, had accused Missy McCain, the captain's mother of taking the medications."

"Did the general express an opinion whether he believed his daughter, Lieutenant?"

"The general said that he was concerned that his daughter had taken the medications either for her own use or for sale, but he could not prove it."

"That being said, Lieutenant, the general nevertheless dismissed Ms. McCain despite the fact that he did not feel she had done anything wrong. Is that right?"

"At a later time, both the general and the defendant confirmed that Lori, the general's daughter that is, threatened to bring charges against Captain McCain for raping her unless Missy McCain were dismissed from her position."

"So, Lieutenant, whether truthful or not, such an allegation would have effectively ended the defendant's career and may well have lead to his being incarcerated. Is that true?"

"Objection," the defense attorney interjected. "Calls for a conclusion from the witness."

"I withdraw the question," the prosecutor stated, having made his point.

The prosecuting attorney asked Carl about Brian's contention that he had been home alone the night of the murder, followed by his admission that he had been off the base during the time when Lori was murdered only after the police confronted him with definitive proof that he had been seen leaving the base by the sentry on duty at the main gate.

"Your Honor, I have no further questions for this witness."

The distinguished defense attorney slowly rose from his chair and approached Carl, who patiently awaited cross examination. Usually, Carl found that the cross was perfunctory, since the defense didn't want to place emphasis on hard evidence which may be harmful to their case. In this case, however, Peter Scott did something totally unexpected. He ran counter to the first thing which is taught in law school—Don't ever ask a witness a question unless you already know what the answer will be. He asked Carl, "Lieutenant, do you believe that my client, Captain McCain, killed Lori Newton?"

Fortunately for Carl, the prosecutor was immediately on his feet. "Objection, Your Honor. This question in uncalled for, and the defense is perfectly aware of this. The question is irrelevant, immaterial, and calls for a conclusion from the witness."

"Sustained, Counselor," the judge responded, whereupon he turned to the defense attorney. "Mr. Scott, I have warned Mr. Levine, and now I am warning you. I will not tolerate this sort of behavior in my court. We will not play games, do you understand?"

"Yes, sir. My apologies to the court, Your Honor."

"Lieutenant, had the St. Louis Police not had Dewayne Foster under surveillance, he, not my client, would be sitting in that chair, is that not true?" as Scott pointed to the seat where Brian was planted.

"I suspect so," Carl responded.

"You more than suspect so, don't you Lieutenant? In fact, Faster Foster was known to have been in cahoots with Lori Newton. We have already heard testimony that there was a falling out, if you will, between the two. Moreover, the DNA of Mr. Foster was found at the scene of the murder. So Mr. Foster certainly had the motive to kill the decedent and there was scientific evidence placing him at the scene."

"Objection, Your Honor." Levine said. "The defense is giving his closing statement with the examination of this witness. If he has a question, he should ask it."

"With all due respect, Your Honor," Scott replied, "it is entirely appropriate to ask Lieutenant Watson, who is the prosecution's witness after all, about other possible interpretations of the evidence they provided."

"Objection overruled, but if you have a question of this witness, Counselor, ask it," the judge admonished.

"Lieutenant," the attorney continued, "is it possible that Mr. Foster could have somehow slipped out of his home unbeknownst to the policemen who were observing him?"

"Mr. Scott, you read the affidavits of both officers as well as I did. I can't comment on their surveillance and I don't know whether Mr. Foster was aware that he was being observed."

"Maybe Mr. Foster is brighter than you thought, Lieutenant. Maybe he did know that he was under surveillance."

"You'll have to ask him that, Counselor," Carl responded.

"Oh, I intend to, Lieutenant, I intend to."

CHAPTER THIRTY—NINE

Dr .Lisa O'Malley was scurrying from one medical crisis to the next. Although she had a cadre of medical students, interns, Internal Medicine residents, and Hematology/Oncology fellows to do the "scut work" which occupied much of the practitioner's day, in reality having so many minions trebled her work, since she was obliged not to use them as peons, but to supervise and teach them. In whatever spare time she had left over, she was also required to do her research. The "Publish or Perish" dictum of academic medicine was pervasive and was the bane of many a young professor. Nonetheless, Lisa felt fortunate that she had a really good Chief Fellow. Kevin Smart was aptly named. He was the best Fellow she had ever had, and he had become a godsend, especially since Lisa's reputation among her peers and within the administration of her department and the medical school had grown. As a result, there were more and more demands on her time.

Being African American and a female to boot had been both an advantage and a disadvantage during her training. On the one hand, being in two recognized "minority groups" had opened some opportunities. In previous generations, African Americans who wanted to attend medical school were largely restricted to historically "black" institutions such as Meharry and Howard Universities. In more recent years, however, traditionally "white" medical schools had opened their doors to minorities, African-American, Asian, Latin, and female. On the other hand, Lisa found that many professors, especially those from the older generation of dog-eat-dog hierarchiel training programs, looked askance at anyone who was female or of color, undoubtedly convinced that "those people" were granted admission to medical school because of quotas rather than because of ability.

The further Lisa advanced in her training, the more pervasive was the feeling of isolation. Each higher step made her feel as though she were under greater, not lesser, scrutiny. As a result, Lisa had always been aloof in her social relationships with her peers. She had no family to speak of: her father left upon Lisa's conception; her mother died of complications of diabetes when Lisa was in college; and she had no siblings. Lisa may have had only superficial relationships away from work, but her patients absolutely loved her. When she was in her element, which was while teaching or caring for her patients, Lisa was animated and engaging.

It was her commitment to her patients, even those who had a lot of "baggage" like Dewayne Foster, that led Lisa to fulfill her promise to Dewayne. As soon as she learned of the presence of an identical twin, Lisa had promised herself that she would track down this potential life saver for her patient. Therefore, as she sat quietly reading the *Post Dispatch* with her morning coffee, her attention was immediately attracted to a summary of a sensational murder trial being conducted downtown. The name, Dewayne Foster, jumped out at her like a snake from a pit.

Lisa rapidly read the article. Of course, she already knew that Dewayne was a drug user. She had suspected that he was also a dealer, but Lisa never made value judgments about her patients. She certainly paid attention to their social needs, but she always treated them with the respect and attention they deserved. What the newspaper article did tell her, however, was the identity of Dewayne Foster's identical twin. It was Brian McCain, the man accused of murder, but also the man who could supply Dewayne with the potentially life-saving stem cells which he may eventually so desperately need.

Lisa perused the article and saw the name of the police officer who was in charge of the investigation. She decided to contact Lieutenant Carl Watson to get more information. Dewayne, she knew, was scheduled for his follow up bone marrow examination that afternoon, and she would speak with him about his twin at that time.

Two days a week, Lisa O'Malley and her fellows had a leukemia clinic, during which time they monitored the status of the dozens of patients with the life-threatening disease. Dewayne Foster was the last patient of the busy day, and it was nearly 5:30 when she saw his blood counts which had been drawn earlier that afternoon. Although Dewayne's nose bleeds and bleeding from his gums had stopped, his platelet count remained only half of the 150,000 count that Lisa would have preferred. His white blood count had gone from a high of nearly 80,000 when she first met him to zero as a result of the aggressive chemotherapy he had needed. That count was now 2300, lower than she expected but still better than before his chemotherapy. The concern Lisa always had in these situations was whether the blood counts remained abnormal because of the treatment or because of an incomplete remission of his acute myelomonocytic leukemia. The bone marrow test would answer that question.

Lisa had performed thousands of bone marrow tests over the years. In fact, she had even let one of her professors do a bone marrow on her when he needed a normal control subject for research he was doing. Lisa justified putting herself through the mildly uncomfortable procedure on the basis of contributing to science, but her real reason for volunteering was so that she could honestly explain to her patients what to expect when they underwent the procedure.

As Dewayne was getting dressed after the procedure was completed, Lisa asked him, "Dewayne, I saw in the paper that you are being called as a witness in a criminal case. Have they told you that they discovered who your identical twin is?"

"No, Doctor O'Malley, I haven't heard anything about it." Dewayne had really grown to like and to respect Lisa, and he treated her with great deference, which was a far cry from how he treated most women, especially African American women.

"It is the man who has been accused of the murder of that woman, Dewayne. His name is Brian McCain."

Faster nearly fell over. "Are you telling me that the army captain is my twin?"

"Yes, Dewayne, that's how they found out. When they discovered that you were home when the girl was killed, they did DNA testing on other people who may have known her, and they found out the captain is your twin. Dewayne, do you have any idea how important that is? Lisa asked.

"What do you mean, Doc?"

"Dewayne, someday you probably will need a stem cell transplant, which is kind of like a bone marrow transplant. Since your bone marrow has had leukemic cells in it, we really can't use your own marrow for what we call an auto-transplant, since your marrow would probably be contaminated with a few residual leukemic cells, even if it looks normal under the microscope. We could use an unrelated donor, but that increases the risk of rejection or graft versus host disease, in which your body reacts against the foreign marrow. By far, the best alternative would be for you to receive the stem cells from an identical twin, since his stem cells would be free of any malignant leukemic cells and there would be virtually no risk of rejection or graft versus host disease."

Dewayne sat pensively and then asked, "When can we do this, Doc? Let's get on with it."

"One step at a time, Dewayne. First we need to see how your bone marrow looks, then we'll decide whether you need a transplant and, if so, the best time to do it. Then, of course we need to get Captain McCain to agree to provide the stem cells."

"What do you mean, agree? Can't we make him do it?"

"No, Dewayne. That is something that only he can agree to, but I can't imagine anyone refusing to help another human being, especially his long lost identical twin." This was to become much more complicated in the next several weeks, however.

CHAPTER FORTY

The following day, the defense opened its case, Peter Scott hoping to convince the jury that there was sufficient reasonable doubt to exonerate his client. The attorney had to believe that the jury was of the opinion that Lori Newton was killed by either Dewayne Foster or his client, Brian McCain. It seemed inconceivable that there was a mysterious third person out there, so unless he could discredit the testimony of Faster Foster and the policemen, his client would probably be convicted.

Scott called Officer James Symington as his first witness. After the prosecutor's questioning of Sergeant Nolan, the policemen who had Dewayne Foster under surveillance , the defense attorney elected not to cross examine him at that time, preferring instead to call Officer Symington, the other officer and the one who seemed to be the more vulnerable of the two, as his own witness. That way, he hoped that the points he made with the witness would be fresher in the minds of the jury.

"Officer Symington, what prompted you and Sergeant Nolan to decide to keep Mr. Foster under surveillance when you already had incriminating evidence against both Lori Newton and him?"

"We were concerned, Counselor, that the fabrication that the two of them came up with, namely that they were collecting toys and money to provide for inner city children, was a bunch of crap. We were afraid they were going to beat the rap, so we wanted to collect more evidence against them."

"Your Honor," Aaron Levine objected, "the state objects to this witness' language. In addition, the response was based on opinion and not on fact."

"Sustained."

"Rephrasing the question, Officer Symington," Scott continued, "were you asked by your superiors to continue the surveillance on Mr. Foster?"

"No, sir, but we were aware that there was concern within the department about the strength of the evidence we had against Mr. Foster and Ms. Newton, so we tried to get additional information."

"Officer, how many entrances, or exits, as the case may be, are there from Mr. Foster's building?"

"There is a main entrance, but Faster always used his private entrance."

"So you and Sergeant Nolan needed to watch both exits continuously from 7:00 p.m. to 2:30 a.m. to prove that he didn't leave the building and then return?"

"That's right, Counselor."

"Officer Symington, did you and Sergeant Nolan drink coffee or soda or water during that seven and a half hours of surveillance? After all, it was quite late, so I assume you were quite tired."

"Yeah, both of us drank a ton of coffee. You know how cops are—coffee and doughnuts," and Symington turned to the jury a sheepish grin on his face.

Aaron Levine shuddered, for he knew exactly where the defense was taking this line of questioning.

"Officer," Scott continued, ready to pounce, "I assume that, because of all the coffee you and Sergeant Nolan drank, that you had to relieve yourselves at some time during that seven and one half hours."

"Sure. We had to pee into an empty Coke bottle, and a couple of times we ducked down an alley and took a leak, just to stretch our muscles, you know. As I get older, you know, my prostate seems to be getting bigger and bigger so I can't hold it like I used to be able to," replied the unsuspecting policeman, still unaware of the upcoming trap.

"So, Officer Symington, is it not true that there were periods of time, several periods of time in fact, during which one or both of you were not watching Mr. Foster's building, and is it not true that during these periods of laxity on your part Mr. Foster could have exited his building, traveled to Forest Park, killed Lori Newton, and returned to his building, only to reenter the building when one or both of you were again 'taking a leak,' as you put it? You don't need to answer the question, Officer," and the attorney retreated to his chair.

The prosecution tried to recoup some of their losses during cross examination, but the damage had been done.

Mr. Scott then called Slower Stoker, Faster's less than bright bodyguard.

"Mr. Stoker, you are under the employ of Mr. Dewayne Foster, is that correct?"

"Yeah, that's right. I do whatever Faster needs me to do, and I look after him."

"You look after him. Tell the Court, Mr. Stoker, why Mr. Foster needs looking after."

113

"Well, sometimes people Faster does business with get upset with him, so I just make sure everything in okay."

"So, Mr. Stoker, you are kind of like a bodyguard for Mr. Foster, is that correct?"

"Yeah, I guess you could say that."

"Mr. Stoker, how long have you known Dewayne Foster?"

"Me and Faster been together since we grew up on the streets years ago."

"So would it be safe to say that you would do anything for Mr. Foster, anything at all?"

"Faster takes care of me, so I would always take care of him."

"Mr. Stoker, were you or Mr. Foster aware of the fact that the police sometimes had him under surveillance, were watching him?"

"Sure," Stoker responded. "We didn't know it when they saw Faster and that blonde talking out in front of the building, but after that we always checked them out. Faster had a bunch of monitors in his place that kept an eye on the neighborhood, using outside cameras, so the cops might as well have been wearing neon."

"Mr. Stoker, on the night in question, were you with Dewayne Foster?"

"No, I was out with my lady. Faster told me he didn't need me that night."

"Was that unusual, Mr. Stoker?" the defense attorney continued.

"Yeah, I don't get many chances to be with my lady, you know?" Slower seemed embarrassed as he turned to face the jury. "Anyway, I usually live in my own place in Faster's building. It is only two or three minutes away from him, and he has a buzzer that he can use to call me anytime."

"Did Mr. Foster ask you to hang around the building that night, Mr. Stoker?"

"Nah. He usually did, but that night I was really surprised. Faster told me to leave the building and go spend it with Mahalia, that's my lady, so I did."

"Would you say, therefore, that Mr. Foster seemed to want you out of the building so that you would not be able to see if he should leave the premises without anyone knowing?"

"Objection, Your Honor!" Levine nearly screamed. "The defense knows this question is inappropriate. It draws a conclusion from the witness."

"Objection sustained," and the judge admonished Peter Scott. "Counselor, you know better." He then turned to the jury and instructed the jury to disregard the last question.

The defense attorney responded with a satisfied, "No further questions,"

114

as he successfully hid his smug smile.

The final witness called by the defense was Dewayne Foster.

"Mr. Foster, we have heard testimony that you and the decedent had a rather heated argument outside your building, an argument during which the decedent became quite incensed about your business relationship, shall we say. Are you aware of that testimony?"

"I didn't hear the testimony, but the cops told me what they heard. They misunderstood. Miss Newton and I were involved in an effort to provide toys and playground equipment for disadvantaged inner city children, nothing more. Lori had quite a temper, and she was upset because I had some questions about the allocation of funds."

"What sort of business enterprises are you involved in, Mr. Foster?"

"I deal with imports and exports."

"Imports and exports from Mexico and Colombia perhaps, Mr. Foster? Imports and exports that are transported under the cover of darkness and without the approval of the DEA perhaps, Mr. Foster?"

"Objection, Your Honor."

"Sustained. Mr. Scott," the judge admonished, "you will avoid side comments in the future, do you understand?"

"Yes, Your Honor."

"Is it not true, Mr. Foster, that you have been arrested three times for distribution of drugs in St. Louis?"

"Those charges were all dismissed."

"Mr. Foster, where were you the night in question?"

"I was home alone the entire evening."

"You never left your home the entire night."

"That's what I said, Counselor."

"Mr. Foster, were you aware that you were under surveillance the night of Lori Newton's murder?"

"Hell, yes, I knew. Those guys were so obvious, only an idiot wouldn't have known they were watching me. The entire neighborhood was laughing about it for a week, because everybody knew. Especially when the cops gave me an ironclad alibi, then we all cracked up. Thank God for the police; you know to Serve and Protect. They certainly served and protected me, didn't they, Counselor?"

Mr. Scott continued, "Mr. Foster, why did you send Mr. Stoker away the night in question? Was it because you wanted to be able to leave your building freely, with no one aware of your departure?"

"I wanted Slower, I mean Rufus, to be able to spend some time with his lady, Counselor. He had been pretty out of sorts lately, you know? Probably was feeling deprived."

As the defense attorney turned to his table to review his notes, he heard a thud from the witness stand. He turned just in time to see Dewayne Foster lying on the floor, his chair overturned. The witness was in the midst of a *grand mal* seizure. As the court erupted in pandemonium, the bailiff quickly ushered the jury out and the judge leaped into action, padding the handle of his gavel with his clean handkerchief and carefully placing it between Dewayne's teeth to prevent him from biting his tongue. He then eased the patient to the floor and placed him on his side in the event Dewayne vomited. Carl quickly went to the judge's side to assist.

"We called 911, Your Honor," Carl said. "Faster has been getting chemotherapy for acute leukemia, you know, and this may be related to that."

"I knew he was ill," the jurist said. "I didn't know any of the details."

Carl opened Dewayne's wallet and located the name and phone number of his hematologist. He then called the number, hoping to alert the physician that her patient would soon be *en route* to Barnes Hospital.

Carl was put through to Lisa O'Malley just as the EMT crew arrived in the courtroom. The techs immediately took over. Dewayne had stopped seizing, but he was still in a post ictal state of confusion and disorientation. They placed an oral airway and politely returned the gavel and handkerchief to the judge.

"Looks like you're going to have a remembrance of this, Judge," one of the techs said as he pointed out the teeth marks deeply etched into the handle of the gavel. "Better the gavel than his tongue, though."

"The EMT team is right here, Dr. O'Malley," Carl reported.

"Let me speak with them, and then I need to talk with you, Lieutenant, if that's okay?"

"Sure, that would be fine," Carl said, but in reality, the physician's sweet, yet controlled, authoritative voice caught Carl's attention. "More than fine," he thought.

"Dr. O'Malley, this is Neil Gray with the St. Louis Fire and Rescue Squad. The current status is that the patient reportedly had a *grand mal* seizure, now resolved. He has no apparent injury nor does he have any lateralizing or focal neurological findings, although he is still post ictal. His oxygen saturation is 94% and his vitals are stable."

"Sounds good, Mr. Gray," Lisa responded. "Transport him ASAP to the

ER at Barnes Hospital. He may have seized because of an electrolyte disorder, but much more likely it is from a CNS infection or leukemic meningitis. Start an IV with D5/water at a TKO rate, please."

"Already done, Doc."

"I should have known," Lisa complimented. "You guys don't need me."

"Thanks, Doc. We'll be there in about 20 minutes, max."

Carl then retrieved his cell phone. "Dr. O'Malley, this is Carl Watson."

"Yes, Lieutenant. Thank you for taking the time to speak with me. Would you please see if Captain McCain's attorney, Mr. Scott, would be available to meet with you and me? I need to speak with both of you as it pertains to my patient's condition."

Carl was perplexed as to how Brian McCain could be related to Dewayne Foster's medical condition, but he said, "Just a moment, please, doctor. Mr. Scott is right here, and I will see what I can arrange."

The three of them set a time later that afternoon when they could meet at the attorney's office. Carl quickly volunteered to pick Lisa up at her office, and to his delight, she accepted his offer.

As Dewayne Foster was wheeled out of the courtroom and into the hallway, Carl observed Rufus Stoker tearfully approach the gurney. Faster appeared frail and vulnerable, with a crisp white sheet covering him such that only his pasty face was visible. The huge man was disconsolate and child-like as he mournfully reached under the sheet and held Faster's hand. Slower then turned to the EMT and said, "You've got to fix him, you've got to."

CHAPTER FORTY—ONE

At four o'clock that afternoon, Carl arrived at Barnes Hospital and was directed to Dr. O'Malley's office. Carl was uncomfortable, and he wasn't sure why. He felt like a teenager on his first date. He had never even met Lisa O'Malley, but the voice on the other end of their brief phone conversation had certainly gotten his attention. Despite his apprehension, Carl smiled to himself, thinking of previous blind dates that had been arranged for him. She'll probably be uglier than sin, or arrogant as hell, he thought, and she is probably married, with two kids.

As Lisa entered the waiting room and approached Carl, he immediately noticed two things. She was certainly not ugly as sin, and she had no wedding band on the thin ring finger of her left hand.

Carl stood and shook her hand. She responded with a firm, confident grip, but one with sensitivity and compassion. Carl had always put a lot of credence in ones handshake, and Lisa O'Malley's stature rose greatly in his eyes with this simple gesture.

"Dr. O'Malley, I am Carl Watson. Very nice to meet you."

"Nice to meet you, too, Lieutenant. I appreciate your picking me up to meet with Mr. Scott. My car is in the shop for some repairs, so I am at a loss for wheels until tomorrow."

The two of them wound their way through the corridors of the busy hospital and entered an oversized elevator car large enough to handle a frail elderly lady on a gurney, a young girl and her doll in a too-large wheelchair, the various attendants, and the two handsome African Americans. One of the nurses smiled broadly at Lisa and teasingly said, "Good afternoon, Dr. O'Malley. I hope you and your friend are able to break away early for dinner out?"

Lisa was embarrassed and somewhat taken back. "This is a business associate of mine, Kathy. Carl Watson, this is Karen Bloemer, one of our great nurses on the Oncology ward." Lisa studiously avoided answering the pretty young nurse's comment about an early dinner, but the thought did cross her mind. Carl, meanwhile, looked sideways at Lisa and smiled.

While walking toward Carl's car, Lisa said, "I am really fortunate to have wonderful nurses on the Oncology ward, and Karen is one of the best."

"She obviously has a lot of respect for you, Doctor," Carl observed.

"I try to be engaged with the nurses, to make sure that I am just part of the team, as they are. The camaraderie goes a long way in helping all of us deal with cancer patients. Sometimes, though, Karen has a tendency to be rather outspoken."

Carl made a spontaneous decision. "Perhaps you would like to have a bite to eat after we meet with Brian's attorney, and I can then deliver you home, since you admitted that you are without your car anyway. You do have to eat sometime, after all."

Lisa turned to Carl, smiled, and said, "We'll see."

When Carl and Lisa arrived at Peter Scott's office in a large downtown St. Louis building, they were ushered into a spacious and opulent office with distinguished mahogany furnishings, a large desk with orderly stacks of paperwork, and a separate grouping consisting of a couch, coffee table, and side chairs. A shiny silver tray held a carafe of coffee, water, and various sodas.

Carl introduced Lisa to Peter Scott, and they all sat in the more informal seating area.

"Thank you for meeting with me so promptly, Mr. Scott," Lisa began. "I wanted to bring you and Lieutenant Watson up to date on my patient's condition and how it may impact your client, or, more accurately, how your client could impact my patient."

Both men sat patiently, still unsure as to where this conversation was headed.

Lisa continued. "Mr. Foster has acute myelomonocytic leukemia, which was universally fatal years ago, but which now, with the advent of new chemotherapy drugs, is a very treatable disease. You notice that I said treatable, rather than curable, although, in certain circumstances cure is possible.

"Mr. Foster has achieved a partial remission with his first course of chemotherapy. A partial remission means that his disease has improved, but his bone marrow is not normal. In addition, we did a spinal tap and an MRI scan of his brain today. These studies do not show evidence of an infection in the brain, which was one of my initial concerns, but he does have leukemic meningitis. The chemotherapy drugs, which are given intravenously, may not effectively penetrate into the brain or the lining of the brain, called the meninges, and the abnormal leukemic cells may take safe harbor in this so-called sanctuary site. As a result, we are going to have to give Mr. Foster

119

additional systemic chemotherapy as well as chemotherapy directly into the spinal canal. If this is effective, he still would be at very high risk of eventually having a relapse of his disease unless he were to undergo a stem cell transplant, and this is where Captain McCain comes into play."

"I am beginning to understand, Dr. O'Malley," Scott said. "Since my client and Mr. Foster are identical twins, you want Captain McCain to provide the stem cells for the transplant."

"Wait a minute," Carl interjected. "I don't understand. Why does Brian have to be the donor? Why not go to the donor pool and find a match? After all, lots of us have been entered into the computer as organ donors, and for this you don't even have to die first to be a donor."

"The reason Captain McCain is the key, Lieutenant," Lisa explained, "is that Mr. Foster cannot be his own donor, even if we are able to achieve a complete remission of his disease, since his own cells would undoubtedly be contaminated by residual leukemic cells. To use a match from the donor pool is problematic for a couple of reasons. First, the pool of African American candidates is much smaller than that of Caucasian donors, so the likelihood of finding a good match is lower. More importantly, even if we did find a good donor candidate, that donor would never be as good as Mr. Scott's client because being an identical twin means that there is virtually no risk of graft versus host disease or rejection."

"What are you asking of my client, Doctor?"

"I'm asking him to agree to provide a blood specimen very similar to the amount of blood that he would provide to the Red Cross for its blood bank. There is minimal discomfort to the donor, except for some mild bone pain for a day or two from a medication we give ahead of time to increase the production of his own stem cells. It is important to understand that there is virtually no risk to the donor."

The attorney turned to Carl. "What do you think, Lieutenant? Despite the fact that you had to arrest him, Brian seems to have a lot of respect for you. Would you be willing to speak with him about this?"

"Me?" Carl exclaimed, obviously surprised at this request.

Lisa turned to Carl. "Lieutenant, if Captain McCain would be willing to speak with you, I would be more than happy to be there with you to answer any of the medical questions he may have."

Although Carl was inclined to agree to Peter Scott's request anyway, the opportunity to spend more time with Lisa O'Malley clinched it. "All right," he said. "If you will be there for moral support, I will speak with Brian."

Carl and Lisa were alone in the elevator as they left the attorney's office. Carl turned to Lisa. "What I should have said is that I would agree to talk to Brian if you would accompany me and if you would agree to dinner this evening, Doctor."

"It would be my pleasure, Lieutenant, but only if you drop the Doctor and call me Lisa."

Carl could sense the gentle palpitations within his chest as he responded, "And I am Carl."

CHAPTER FORTY—TWO

Carl slept more soundly that night than he had in weeks, if not months. His dinner with Lisa had been a sheer delight, from his standpoint, and it appeared as though she found it equally enjoyable. Lisa had already made arrangements to get a ride to work the following day, but Carl had offered to pick her up that afternoon so they could drive to Fort Leonard Wood and explain the situation to Brian. Meanwhile, she had asked one of her peers to cover her outpatient clinic that day.

The drive to the army base was very relaxed and comfortable. The typical humidity of a Midwest summer had abated, and the day was sunny and mild. Carl had learned that Lisa, like him, had no family remaining. The difference, however, was that Carl had never known any family. Lisa, at least, had a long term relationship with her mother prior to her mother's death. By the time their dinner and their subsequent car trip were over, both of them felt as though they had known the other for months, if not years, rather than a mere 24 hours.

Brian had been relieved of his military duties pending resolution of the criminal trial, so he spent most of his day aimlessly walking alone in the hills around the base or reading in his living quarters. He had never been a particularly social person, and his current notoriety made him even more desirous of being alone. He had obviously lost weight during his tribulations, and his complexion was now ashen and blotchy. Nonetheless, he greeted Carl warmly.

"Brian, this is Dr. Lisa O'Malley. She is the hematologist who is caring for Dewayne Foster."

"Pleased to meet you, Doctor. However, I must admit that I was perplexed when Carl called and said that you wanted to meet with me."

"I will try to explain it to you, Captain," and Lisa proceeded to educate Brian as to the concept of partial remission, complete remission, relapse, leukemic meningitis, stem cell transplants—indeed, all of the things she had discussed with Carl and Peter Scott the day before.

Brian was obviously a very bright person, and he immediately grasped where the discussion was headed. In fact, he preempted Lisa's request that he consider being a stem cell donor by interjecting, "And I suspect that you want me to contribute my bone marrow to help save the man who killed Lori Newton, the man who is running free while I am fighting for my freedom and maybe my life."

Carl was somewhat surprised at the vehemence with which Brian responded to Lisa. Lisa calmly replied, "Captain, first, my patient is not 'running free.' In fact, he is absolutely fighting for his life, even more so than are you. And I am not asking you to donate your bone marrow. I am asking you to donate your stem cells, which is much easier on you and which offers you virtually no risk and very minimal discomfort."

Brian didn't reply, but got up from his chair and walked around the small, but neatly arranged, room. "Doctor, Lori Newton threatened to destroy my career. More importantly, she did destroy my mother's hopes and dreams, and it is very likely that she killed my mother—actually killed her. She has wreaked havoc on everyone and everything around her—her father, her sister, me, my mother , all those people she was providing with drugs—everyone. Am I sad that Lori Newton is dead? Absolutely not. But I would never have killed her. That being said, the evidence tells us that there are only three possible explanations of who may have killed her. I could have done it, according to the DNA and my lack of an alibi, but I know that I didn't do it; so that possibility doesn't exist. Secondly, a mysterious third person could have done it, but that seems inconceivable, given the DNA evidence, which is irrefutable; so that possibility also is excluded. Therefore, the only remaining explanation is that Dewayne Foster did it. He certainly had motive, and the evidence suggests that he should be the prime suspect. His alibi, as it is, is easily explained away by the inattention of the police officers as Mr. Scott pointed out."

Brian became even more animated as he continued. "Why would I ever want to help the man who is trying to put me in prison? Tell me, why?"

Lisa remained calm. "Captain, I could never fully grasp the emotions which you must be feeling because only you are in the position that you are, but you ask why you would want to help Dewayne Foster. I'll tell you why; because he is a human being with a heart and a soul, and you are in a unique position in that you, and only you, can help this fellow human being. Not only that, he is your brother, your identical twin. You developed side by side in your mother's uterus, so you must have some sense of identity with him."

"Doctor," Brian replied, "you said that Dewayne Foster has a heart and a soul. He has a heart of stone and the soul of the devil. His entire life has been directed toward Dewayne Foster and only Dewayne Foster. He has poisoned

123

the lives and souls of uncounted people, mostly vulnerable people, and he has no remorse. He could rot in hell as far as I am concerned. We may be identical twins, Doctor, because we share strands of genetic material, but that is all that we share."

Brian felt spent. He was overwhelmed with emotion, and Lisa sensed that further discussion at this time would be counterproductive at best, so she quietly said, "Captain, I am sure that you are reeling right now, and I do feel bad about complicating your life. All I ask is that you consider what we talked about, and Carl and I will talk to you about it in a few days."

Brian nodded absently. "I will consider it, Doctor, but don't get your hopes up."

CHAPTER FORTY—THREE

Carl and Lisa silently drove through the rolling foothills on their way back to St. Louis, their upbeat attitude on their way to see Brian McCain now replaced by the realization that Brian might turn down Lisa's request. Although Carl had mixed feelings about Brian donating his stem cells for Faster, he was hopeful that Brian would eventually agree, for Lisa's sake more than for Faster's.

Carl's cell phone chirped, and he reached to his hip and answered the call, assuming it would be Mouse or someone from the office with another crisis to be managed. Surprisingly, the caller said, "Carl, this is Brian. Are you and Dr. O'Malley on your way back to St. Louis?"

"Yes, Brian, she is here with me, and we are approaching the city now." Carl gestured to Lisa as he mouthed to her, "It's Brian." She raised her eyebrows with equal surprise, since neither of them expected to hear back from Brian this quickly.

"Carl, I have thought about what the doctor said, and I have a proposition for her patient. Carl, I know for a fact that I am innocent of killing Lori, and I know just as strongly that Foster killed her. Tell him that if he confesses to killing Lori, then, and only then, I will donate my stem cells for his transplant. His life for mine, Carl, it's as simple as that."

"I'll tell Dr. O'Malley, Brian, and she can tell Faster what you said."

"And Carl, on a lighter note, the way the two of you look at each other says volumes. If you don't pick up on the good doctor, you are out of your mind."

Carl smiled and said, "I'll take that under consideration, Captain."

Carl then hung up and related Brian's offer to Lisa. "Carl, I don't know if I can ethically present that to Dewayne. It's almost like extortion. You confess, even if you didn't do it, and I will give you my stem cells, which may save your life."

"Lisa, it's not extortion if Dewayne actually killed Lori, which, by the way, I think he did. I don't blame Brian."

Lisa just shook her head. "You talk about convoluted. When people say truth is stranger than fiction, they aren't exaggerating. I'll talk to Dewayne about what Brian offered."

"Why don't we stop somewhere for dinner. Lisa? I'm getting hungry."

"Carl, I'm beat. Tell you what. I've got the fixings for my world famous Cajun pasta at my house, complete with a bottle of red wine from Napa Valley. Why don't you come in and I will actually feed you?"

"That sounds like a great idea," Carl enthusiastically answered.

Carl had not had a homemade dinner provided for him for as long as he could remember, but it was well worth the wait, he thought, as he helped Lisa rinse the dishes before putting them into the dishwasher. Carl felt as though they were a newly married couple as they cleaned up the kitchen side-by-side. They then retired to the living room, wine glasses in hand. Carl leaned back on the comfortable mocha leather sofa and put his stockinged feet up on the coffee table. To his delight, Lisa sat down right next to him on the large curvilinear couch and leaned into him as they listened to Harry Connick, Jr., crooning from the Bose.

"I feel 10,000 miles from the worries of the hospital right now," Lisa purred.

"I know exactly how you feel, Lisa. I haven't been this relaxed for as long as I can remember. It must be the wine."

Lisa gazed romantically at Carl and said, "I don't know about you, but for me, it's not the wine, it's the company."

Carl then carefully lowered his feet and put both of their wine glasses on the coffee table. He turned to Lisa and they embraced, followed by a kiss so sweet and gentle that Carl thought he would melt into the sofa.

Lisa could sense his smile and asked, "A penny for your thoughts."

"I was thinking how kissing you was one of the most pleasurable things I have ever done."

"My feeling exactly," Lisa responded, and they kissed again, this time with more urgency.

The following morning, Lisa slipped quietly got out of bed and headed for the shower. She had the coffee brewing and breakfast ready when Carl, freshly showered but wearing his day old clothes, entered the kitchen. A quick kiss later, she said, "Can you take me by the auto shop so I can pick up my car? I feel lost without my wheels."

"Be happy to."

"I need to check in on Dewayne first thing this morning. I'll call you later and let you know what he says."

CHAPTER FORTY—FOUR

Dewayne Foster had been seizure free since arriving at the hospital. Kevin Smart, Lisa's cracker-jack Chief Fellow had already arranged for the surgeons to implant an Omaya reservoir under the scalp. This would facilitate the direct instillation of chemotherapy into the cerebrospinal fluid which surrounds the brain and the spinal canal, the most effective means for treating leukemic meningitis. Meanwhile, additional systemic chemotherapy had been started to try to get Dewayne into a complete remission.

Lisa entered her patient's room. He had not yet been placed on isolation because his blood counts were still acceptable, but she had told Dewayne that he would require isolation within the next day or two. Rufus Stoker, Dewayne's man-Friday was again sitting quietly in the room. Lisa told Dewayne that she needed to speak with him about a possible transplant. When asked if he wanted Rufus to step out, Faster responded, "No, Slower can stay. We don't have any secrets from each other, do we, Slower?"

"No, boss. No secrets."

Lisa again explained to Dewayne that he would require a stem cell transplant, but only if he were able to achieve a complete remission, both in his bone marrow and in his spinal fluid. Otherwise, a transplant would be all for naught. She then reviewed what they had discussed before: that Brian McCain, who was his identical twin, would be the most appropriate donor, since that would reduce the risk of graft versus host disease or rejection.

"Will he do that?" Dewayne bluntly asked. "I mean, I'm not his favorite person right now."

"He'll do it, boss, or I'll beat the shit out of him!" Slower exclaimed as he jumped from his seat. His reaction caught Lisa unaware, since she had forgotten that he was even in the room.

"Sit down, Slower. He'll do it, won't he, Doc?"

"Dewayne, Captain McCain is under a lot of stress right now. He insists that he is innocent, and he is equally convinced that you are the one who killed Lori Newton."

"That's a lie," Slower roared, "a goddamn lie!"

"Easy, Slower," Dewayne said, trying to calm the big man down. "Go ahead, Doc, will he give me the cells or not?"

"What he said, Dewayne, is that he will donate his stem cells only if you confess to killing Lori Newton. If you won't confess, he said he would refuse to donate."

"But I didn't kill her. I'm not going to confess to something I didn't do, just to get his damn cells, and the transplant may not work anyway. You told me that yourself, Doc."

"That's right, Dewayne, there is no guarantee that the stem cell transplant will help, but those are his conditions. I don't know who is guilty and who isn't. All I know is that if the chemotherapy doesn't work or if you don't get that transplant you will probably die from your leukemia."

"I'll tell you what you can tell Brian McCain, Doc. No deal. I didn't kill Lori Newton, and I'm not going to say that I did, because I didn't."

CHAPTER FORTY—FIVE

The following week, the trial of *State of Missouri versus Brian McCain* resumed. Peter Scott had decided against calling Brian as a witness, since that would open him up to cross examination by the prosecution, and the defense attorney felt as though his case was strong enough without Brian testifying. He therefore rested his case, and the Judge called for closing arguments.

"Ladies and gentlemen of the jury," Aaron Levine began, "first of all, I want to thank all of you for taking time out of your lives to perform this important civic duty that separates us from nearly all the countries in the world, the duty to represent a jury of our peers.

"I realize that this case is fraught with emotion and is quite confusing," he continued, "but, very simply, it can be summarized as follows. Lori Newton, the decedent, was not a nice person. She was manipulative, deceitful, and hurt nearly everyone who came in contact with her. But Lori Newton did not deserve to be murdered," he emphasized.

"You have heard testimony that the decedent caused the defendant's mother to be dismissed from her job—to be fired from the house and home where she had actually raised Lori Newton as one of her own after the untimely death of Lori's own mother from cancer. The defendant learned of this traitorous behavior on the part of Lori Newton. Not only that, the defendant learned that Lori Newton threatened to destroy his own career by making false accusations against him, accusations which never came forth only because the defendant's mother acquiesced to the threats from the decedent. Brian McCain, the defendant, therefore had personal motives to wish harm to come to Lori Newton. He also had professional reasons to with her harm, namely, his discovery that Lori Newton was intimately involved with the provision of illicit drugs to the soldiers at Fort Leonard Wood, soldiers who were the responsibility of Brian McCain and his surrogate father and mentor, General Frank Newton. Despite these motives, however, I repeat: Lori Newton did not deserve to be murdered. Prosecuted for her crimes, yes; loathed, yes; maybe even despised, yes; but not murdered."

The prosecutor gazed at each of the jurors, and then he resumed his closing statement.

"We now know that the defendant had motive to kill this young lady, at least sufficient motive in his own tormented mind. You also heard testimony that the defendant had the opportunity to kill the decedent. He initially lied to the police when he reported that he was home alone the night of the murder. It was only after there was irrefutable evidence, provided by the sentry at Fort Leonard Wood that Brian McCain was off base during the time that Lori Newton was killed, that the defendant then admitted that he had conveniently forgotten that he had gone for a drive, all alone, in the wee hours of the morning.

"The most damning evidence, however, ladies and gentlemen, comes from the forensics lab, which confirms unequivocally that either the defendant or his previously unknown identical twin was strategically placed in the back seat of the defendant's car in a position where Dr. Boyle, the Medical Examiner, states the assailant was when he attacked, strangled, and killed Lori Newton. Now, Mr. Scott, the defendant's attorney will probably contend that it was Mr. Dewayne Foster, the defendant's identical twin, who lurked in the back seat of that car, but you have also heard testimony from not one, but two, police officers who stated that Dewayne Foster was in his home the entire time during which Lori Newton was killed.

"Ladies and gentlemen," the prosecutor summarized, "Brian McCain had motive and opportunity to have killed Lori Newton, and the evidence placing him at the scene is conclusive. The law would say that you should therefore find him guilty of second degree murder. Thank you." He then turned to the prosecutor's table and sat down.

The judge turned to the jury and said, "Ladies and gentlemen, since it is now nearing the noon hour, we will adjourn until two o'clock, at which time the defense will present its closing argument."

130

CHAPTER FORTY—SIX

Promptly at two o'clock, Peter Scott confidently rose from his chair and approached the jury.

"Ladies and gentlemen, I, too, wish to thank you for your attention during this trial. Particularly, however, I wish to thank you for what I know will be very thoughtful reflection upon the evidence which has been presented to you.

"The prosecutor has described the decedent as a despicable individual who engendered distrust and even loathing, in his words. He then went on to explain that it was the character of the decedent which offered the motive for my client to harm the decedent. What he didn't point out, however, is the very important fact that there were many other people who had a motive to see harm come to Lori Newton—all of those same people with whom she came into contact on a regular basis. We heard testimony that she and Dewayne Foster, the same Dewayne Foster whose DNA was present at the scene of the crime, had an intense argument shortly before she was killed. We heard testimony that she was providing drugs to soldiers at Fort Leonard Wood, and any one of these soldiers, or any one of the people with whom she had drug dealings—the middlemen, if you will—may well have had a motive to kill her. Indeed, her own father, whose career would be at risk if the allegations against his daughter were proven, theoretically would have a motive to harm her. Am I implying that her father killed her? Absolutely not! But what I am saying is that there are any number of people who did not care for Lori Newton and who would wish her harm.

"The prosecutor also contends that my client had opportunity to commit this crime because he was seen leaving the base prior to the time of the crime, but there is no one who can place my client at the scene of the crime. My client was under considerable stress because of the influx of drugs to the base. He has no wife or family with whom he could share his concerns and frustrations, so it is entirely logical that he might want to get away from the base and away from his solitary living quarters for a few hours. I am sure that all of you, ladies and gentlemen, have had times in your lives when the stresses of daily living have caused you to want to get away from it all for a few hours, if you know what I mean"

He paused momentarily to allow the jury to ponder those times in their lives when they may have been able to identify with Brian, and he then continued.

"Let's reconsider who else may have had the opportunity, as the prosecutor referred to it, to kill Lori Newton. Dewayne Foster, for example, certainly would have as much of an opportunity as my client, for example, were it not for the surveillance of two police officers, surveillance, I remind you, that was tainted by the fact that the officers themselves admit that there were periods of time during which they were on a bathroom break during which Mr. Foster could easily have slipped away without their knowledge.

"Finally," the attorney concluded, "Dr. Boyle, the Medical Examiner, has testified that the forensic evidence found at the scene is entirely explicable by the presence of the same Dewayne Foster who had equal motive and opportunity as my client."

"Ladies and gentlemen, the judge will remind you during his instructions to you that if you have reasonable doubt as to the possibility that someone other than my client may have perpetrated this crime, you are then obliged to return a verdict of Not Guilty. As I said at the beginning of my summation, I thank you for your thoughtful deliberation regarding the facts in this case. I now would propose that after such thoughtful deliberation you will undoubtedly conclude that there is more than reasonable doubt as to my client's role in this crime. Therefore, it is your duty to acquit my client. Thank you."

The jury was then given instructions by the judge and excused to begin their deliberation.

CHAPTER FORTY—SEVEN

Peter Scott had always felt that the judicial process was weighted in favor of the prosecution for the simple reason that the average juror enters the jury box with the presumption that the State would not have brought this case to trial unless the evidence for conviction were overwhelming. Therefore, a presumption of innocence was a fallacy. In fact, he felt that most jurors began the trial with a presumption of guilt.

That being said, his corollary assumption was that a quick verdict tended towards one of guilt. If the jury deliberated a longer period of time, in his mind he interpreted that as a sign that there was doubt and conflict within the jury room.

As the hours rolled by and the jury still had not reached a conclusion, Scott felt more and more confident, a confidence bolstered when the bailiff presented a note to the judge asking for a definition of "reasonable doubt." As he and Aaron Levine stood before the judge when the question from the jury was relayed to them, Levine's shoulders notably fell, since it was equally clear to him that this was not a favorable sign for his case.

Peter tried to keep Brian's spirits up with his optimistic interpretation of the events, but with each passing hour, Brian's anxiety level rose and his hopes faded further. He became even more concerned, as did his counselor, when the bailiff brought a second question before the court. "Are we allowed to consider a lesser count, such as manslaughter, instead of second degree murder?" the note read, and the jury also asked for a definition of the different levels of manslaughter to be considered, if this were an option.

The judge consulted with the two attorneys to decide how to answer this unexpected question. Aaron Levine, however, insisted on consulting his boss, Robert Jameson, before making a recommendation, despite the fact that Mr. Jameson had not been present at any of the proceedings, including his Chief Deputy's closing argument, which the State's Attorney had promised to attend.

Levine had strongly suggested to Jameson that they put second degree manslaughter on the table, especially since the Deputy was not at all confident that they would get a guilty verdict on murder two. Jameson, however, made this decision, like most of his decisions, not on facts of law or perceptions of what the jury might do, but rather on politics. His thinking was that if the State won the case, it would be a feather in his cap, but if they lost, he had distanced himself sufficiently that he could cast the blame elsewhere. On the other hand, if he agreed to consideration of second degree manslaughter, he was afraid this would be interpreted as his being "soft on crime." Therefore, the prosecution told the judge that they would not consider a lesser charge.

The jury, having received these new instructions from the judge but unaware of the background reasons for the decision, returned to their deliberations. By the end of the afternoon, they informed the judge that they had not yet reached a decision, so they were sequestered for the night, with further deliberation to begin at 10:00 the following morning.

Another day went by, still with no decision, and everyone's patience was wearing thin. Finally on the third day, the bailiff returned with a note stating that the jury was hopelessly deadlocked. The judge brought the jury into the court and asked whether there was any possibility of reaching a consensus through further discussion or clarification. The jury foreman, a thoughtful middle-aged high school government teacher, replied, "Your Honor, we all respect the court's time and the effect that prolonging this decision has on all the parties involved, especially the defendant; but we are split 8-4 in favor of the defendant, and I don't see how we can ever resolve the differences within the jury."

"Madame Foreperson," the judge asked, "you are sure that you are unable to reach a conclusion?"

"Yes, Your Honor, we are sure."

"Therefore," the jurist declared, with a sense of resignation in his voice, "I have no choice but to declare a mistrial, with my thanks to the jury. Mr. McCain is released on his own recognizance. Mr. Levine, you may consult with Mr. Jameson and determine whether you want to bring this case back to the court, but I would remind you of the vote within the jury room."

"I understand, Your Honor," Levine quietly responded.

CHAPTER FORTY—EIGHT

The next several weeks passed very quickly for Carl Watson. He had a huge backlog of paper work to catch up on since he had been so preoccupied with the McCain/Newton case—paper work which he despised but which, nevertheless, needed to be taken care of.

Carl was relieved that Brian had not been convicted, since he was convinced of Brian's innocence. Meanwhile, the State's Attorney office had been notably quiet about the case, and Carl had heard through the rumor mill that Jameson had no intention of resurrecting this case. He apparently felt it was a scarlet letter on his reputation, and he was just relieved the whole episode seemed to have been forgotten. Some of Carl's sources in the prosecutor's office told him, however, that Jameson was absolutely furious at Aaron Levine about his handling of the case, but Jameson was enough of a realist to understand that he needed Levine to be his front man, since Jameson himself was totally useless in dealing with the nuts and bolts of criminal justice. As a result, the Chief Deputy would survive another of his boss's outrages, as he had many times in the past.

The only person with whom Carl shared his relief about Brian's fate was Lisa. The two of them were spending much more time together, and it was obvious that a serious relationship was developing. It was as if the two of them had put their lives on hold for all those years during which their entire being revolved around their work, but once they discovered each other, a whole new universe had opened for them.

Even Mouse had noticed a dramatic change in Carl since he had met Lisa. Carl had always studiously avoided any social activities with his co-workers, but he even consented to have Lisa and him meet Mouse and his wife for dinner. Carl had serious reservations about how the intellectual, goal-focused Lisa would interact with Mouse's sexpot of a wife, but the dinner was actually very relaxing and enjoyable.

On the way back to Lisa's apartment, Lisa brought up the subject of Dewayne McCain. Although both of them were consummate professionals and never discussed individual names with the other, they nevertheless would, at the end of the day, share generalities of the events of the day. This "venting," they both realized, was therapeutic, something that they each relished.

"Carl," Lisa said, "Dewayne's leukemia appears to be doing well. His latest spinal fluid examination is clear of any leukemic cells, and his bone marrow is recovering very nicely from his re-induction chemotherapy. I will do another bone marrow next week to see if he has achieved a complete remission. If he has, Carl, we need to convince Brian McCain to provide his stem cells for Dewayne. Would you speak with him again and see whether he has changed his mind?"

"Of course I will, Lisa. Maybe, now that it appears he is off the hook for Lori's murder and has been reinstated at the base, he may be more receptive to the idea."

Carl called Brian the following day. "Brian, this is Carl. How are you getting along?"

"As well as can be expected, Carl. Thanks for asking."

"Brian, it looks as though repeat charges will not be filed against you, which I'm sure your attorney has explained to you. I don't need to tell you how happy I am that this whole ordeal turned out like it has. I was never convinced, Brian, that you were guilty. I hope you understand that."

"I do, Carl, and I appreciate it. I know you were in an uncomfortable position because you had a job to do, but I did feel all along that you were supportive of me."

"Brian, as you may or may not know, Lisa O'Malley and I have been seeing quite a bit of each other recently."

"I had presumed that, Carl, watching how the two of you mooned over each other whenever you were within 100 yards of each other."

"It was that obvious, huh?"

"Yes, unless I were deaf, dumb, and blind."

"Anyway, Brian, Lisa told me that it looks as though Dewayne Foster's leukemia is doing pretty well, for now at least. She is going to do some more tests next week, but she is hopeful that his leukemia is in remission."

"I know where you are headed with this, Carl."

"I thought you would. Even if he is in remission, Brian, Dewayne is doomed unless he gets a transplant. Even then, he could still relapse, but at least he would have a chance. Now that the trial is over and you have been exonerated, Lisa was hopeful that you would reconsider being Dewayne's donor, and I feel the same way she does."

"The trial is over, Carl, but I have not been exonerated. I wasn't found not guilty. Dewayne Foster hasn't been convicted. Even though you and my

136

attorney tell me that the ordeal is over, I still feel as though I have this sword hanging over me, just waiting for it to plunge downward. If Dewayne Foster admits to his guilt, I'll do it; that's as much as I can promise you right now. Sorry, Carl."

CHAPTER FORTY—NINE

Carl had told Lisa of his conversation with Brian, of course, but she decided not to share it with her patient until she confirmed that he was indeed in complete remission. The following week, Dewayne Foster had his final biweekly infusion of chemotherapy into his Omaya reservoir, and a sample of the spinal fluid confirmed that his leukemic meningitis had responded to treatment. He also had a follow- up bone marrow examination, and the sophisticated evaluation confirmed a molecular and hematologic complete remission.

Lisa strode into the examination room. As he always was, Rufus Stoker sat quietly in the corner, looking more and more like a bored sumo wrestler.

"Dewayne," Lisa began, "I have some really good news for you. Both your bone marrow and your spinal fluid confirm that your leukemia is now in remission. We are now looking for a good match for your stem cell transplant, and, if we can find a suitable donor, we want to proceed with that within the next month, at the latest."

"Doc, we already know who the best donor would be. It's Brian McCain."

"I realize that, Dewayne, but Lieutenant Watson spoke with him last week and he still refuses. We can't legally force him to do this."

Slower Stoker jumped from his chair. "I'll get him to do it, I guarantee it!" he bellowed.

Lisa was uncomfortable at the behemoth's outburst as Dewayne quietly tried to calm the big man down. "Easy, Slower. We'll figure something out."

Lisa told her patient that she had already begun the process to identify an alternative donor, but she was fully aware that the likelihood of finding an acceptable match was not very great, given the statistics within the African-American patient population. Even if she did find a donor, he would never be as good as Brian McCain.

The following day, Carl received an unexpected call from Fort Leonard Wood. "Carl, this is Brian McCain."

"Yes, Brian, what can I do for you?"

"It's what I can do for you, Carl, or, more literally, what I can do for Dewayne Foster. I thought about what you told me last week and about what

Dr. O'Malley had told me before. I also spent a long time discussing this with General Newton. As you know, I have a tremendous amount of respect for the general, and I value his opinion. In a nutshell, Carl, I have reconsidered and have decided that I will donate stem cells to Dewayne."

Carl was ecstatic. "I'll let Lisa know, Brian, and, trust me, you are making the right decision."

Carl then called Lisa and gave her the good news. "Carl, that is great news. I really appreciate everything you did to help make this happen, and I will appropriately reward you when we are alone," she responded, with a mischievous note of promise in her voice.

Carl smiled and said, "I intend to hold you to that, Doctor; believe me."

Lisa added, "Seriously, Carl, I think it would be best if Brian met with Dewayne to offer his donation face to face. Would he do that, do you think?"

"I don't see why he wouldn't. I'll set it up."

Brian was initially somewhat reluctant to meet with Dewayne, but he finally agreed to do so if Carl and Lisa were present; so arrangements were made to meet the following afternoon in Lisa's office.

Brian left the base shortly after lunch the following day and drove to Lisa's office, unaware that a nondescript gray sedan dogged him the entire way. Brian parked his car in the mammoth multi-level parking garage across Kingshighway from the Medical Office Building which housed the Hematology department. Carl, as arranged, awaited Brian just outside the busy entrance to the building.

"Thanks for coming, Brian. I said it before and I'll say it again. You are doing the right thing, just as you have always done the right thing throughout your entire life, I am sure. That is why I never could accept the possibility that you killed Lori."

The heartfelt declaration was interrupted when a mountain of a man grabbed Brian by the arm and roughly twisted him around. Rufus Stoker had a gun in his massive paw, and he yelled at Brian. "You could save him, but you won't, you bastard!" and he pulled the trigger. Brian collapsed to the floor of the busy atrium, people screaming and fleeing the scene unfolding in front of them. Slower fled from the scene, but Carl's entire attention was focused upon the dead body before him, bleeding on the exquisite tile floor. Carl quickly regained his composure and called his office to arrange for the apprehension of Rufus Stoker.

CHAPTER FIFTY

The next several weeks flew by in a blur. Rufus Stoker, of course, was picked up within a matter of minutes of the shooting. He was arraigned and languished in the County Jail, awaiting a slam dunk conviction, much to the delight of Robert Jameson. Lisa O'Malley had struggled unsuccessfully thus far to locate a potential stem cell donor for Dewayne Foster. She was acutely aware of the short window of opportunity to proceed with the transplant; otherwise her patient would inevitably relapse, and salvage chemotherapy would undoubtedly be futile.

The funeral for Brian McCain had been held several days after the shooting. Carl and Lisa had attended, both of them harboring questions of what might have transpired had Slower Stoker been aware of Brian's purpose for being at Lisa's office that fateful morning. Carl was particularly introspective and quiet, but Lisa just attributed this to the whirlwind that he had been on for the past months.

The relationship between Carl and Lisa continued to flourish, both of them recognizing that this was a commitment that they cherished. In fact, Carl had all but moved in with Lisa, and there had been some talk of getting married in the near future.

Mouse, Fogarty, and Carl had several discussions about the Newton case. Although the case was officially closed, since one suspect was dead, and the other suspect had medical issues which would probably prohibit him from ever being charged, it was still unclear as to who really had killed Lori Newton.

"If you had to bet money, Carl, who do you think did it?" Mouse asked.

Carl though for about a millisecond. "There is no doubt in my mind, Mouse. Faster did it. I know those two cops had him under surveillance, but Faster must have figured some way to get by them without them knowing. Maybe he had another exit, I don't know. He admitted that he knew they were watching him, so he could have figured some way out. And what a perfect alibi—'I couldn't have done it because the cops were watching me.' We'll probably never know for sure, though, unless Faster confesses on his deathbed, and I doubt he would do that."

Carl and Lisa had much the same discussion. Carl knew that Lisa would keep their conversations private, just as she knew he would not share her conversations about her practice, so neither of them kept secrets from the other. Well, Carl thought, almost no secrets.

CHAPTER FIFTY—ONE

When Carl first entered the humble abode of Missy McCain that summer day, little did he realize how the lives of so many people would change, including his own. As he read her journal entries over the next days, facts about Carl's own life began to make sense. Against his better judgment, he began his own journal on that fateful June day.

Journal entry, Carl Watson, June 28, 2008
Called out to an apparent accidental death today, but found a stack of journals which are interesting. An entry from exactly 36 years ago today, my birth date, said that the decedent had delivered at the old City Hospital, where I was born. An entry from a few days later said that she had more than one baby, probably twins, but she only took one baby home and left the other for adoption. Met with Brian McCain, the decedent's son. He is unaware of any siblings. What happened to the other kid?

Journal entry, Carl Watson, July 3, 2008
Went through records from City Hospital buried in the archives at the Clerk's office and found the records re: Missy McCain. She didn't have twins, she had triplets, two of whom were identical and one was non-identical, fraternal, all boys. Her journal said she was gang raped, so the identical twins probably came from one ovum and the other from another, maybe with two different fathers. Found foot prints of all three. Took prints from the non-identical triplet to the Crime Lab. Confirmed that the foot print of the baby matches my prints. I am the third kid. Missy McCain is my mother and Brian McCain is my brother. Wonder what happened to the third of the triplets?
Brian McCain told me that his mother was dismissed because of threats from Lori Newton to accuse him of rape if her father didn't fire Missy McCain. What a bitch!

Journal entry, Carl Watson, July 5, 2008
It looks like Lori Newton killed Missy McCain—not an accident. Somehow need to prove it.

Journal entry, Carl Watson, July 5, 2008

Interviewed Lori Newton. She is a cool customer. She had an explanation for all the evidence. I'm afraid she would skate away from any murder charges. I have got to stop her before she destroys more lives.

Journal entry, Carl Watson, July 7, 2008

It worked like a charm. I planted the bloody snot that I got from Faster Foster's bathroom on the head rest of Lori Newton's car when I strangled her. I never thought I could go through with killing her, but she killed my mother, tried to destroy my brother's life and his career, and is providing drugs for God knows how many soldiers. I figure I got two birds with one stone, implicating Foster.

Journal entry, Carl Watson, July 11, 2008

The ME confirms that Foster's DNA is identical to that found at the scene. That scumball is toast.

Journal entry, Carl Watson, July 15, 2008

Oh, shit. How was I to know that the cops were still watching Foster? He has an alibi, but we still have the DNA. Got to somehow break his alibi. Maybe they lost him during the surveillance.

Journal entry, Carl Watson, July 29, 2008

I don't believe it. Dewayne Foster and Brian McCain are identical twins, so Foster is the third of the triplets. He is my goddamn other brother. Worse, I set him up for the murder and now Brian is a suspect.

Journal entry, Carl Watson, September 7, 2008

Brian's attorney did a great job in discounting Foster's alibi. I think Brian may get off. If he doesn't, somehow I will protect him.

Journal entry, Carl Watson, October 20, 2008

I wish I had never seen my mother's journal. If I hadn't, Brian would still be alive.

EPILOGUE

Rufus Stoker was convicted of the murder of Brian McCain, Robert Jameson didn't run for reelection, since he set his sights higher and was voted in as a Missouri State Senator,   Aaron Levine was elected the new State's Attorney. Dewayne Newton relapsed and died from complications of his acute leukemia, never having received a transplant. Carl Watson took the multiple volumes of Missy McCain's journal as well as his own journals and burned them all.   Lisa O'Malley was promoted to full Professor and was named Chairperson of the Department of Hematology. She and Carl were married and moved to a comfortable house in the South County.

On a mild, idyllic spring day, Carl and Lisa were having a glass of wine on the deck of their new home as they reflected on the entire McCain/Newton affair.

"You know, Honey," Lisa began, "it's sad that Lori Newton destroyed so many lives—Brian's, Brian's mother's, her own father's. I hate to say it, being a healer by nature, but it's just as well that she died."

Carl became very pensive. "You may be right, Lisa," he said as he approached her from behind and held her tightly.   "If this whole ugly mess hadn't unfolded as it did, have you ever thought that we might never have met? I remember one time Brian said that in the military, they are always concerned about collateral damage. In civilian life, I call them unintended consequences. At least one good unintended consequence came out of this mess. "

"Oh we would have met," Lisa responded, and she turned and kissed him.

About the Author

E.C. Hoppin, M.D., practiced as a Hematologist/Oncologist for thirty-two years, including eighteen as Medical Director of a Midwestern cancer center, before serving as a Chief Medical Officer. He graduated from the University of California at Berkeley and St. Louis University School of Medicine. His post graduate training was at the University of California at Davis/Sacramento Medical Center. Dr. Hoppin is the author of several scientific publications and the non-fiction, *The Joy of Cancer.* He and his wife reside in downstate Illinois, near their two adult sons, daughters-in-law, and granddaughter.

Dr. Hoppin may be contacted at hoppin@consolidated.net.

www.ingramcontent.com/pod-product-compliance
Lightning Source LLC
Chambersburg PA
CBHW071306130626
46556CB00004B/1483